Unwanted

Devilish #5

Charity Parkerson

Punk & Sissy Publications

Copyright

Contents

Introduction

Two entities have Fen on their radar. He only knows about one. That's a blindness that might get him killed.

After Fen's abduction, Celeste wiped his memory. He has no idea what happened to him after Jörmungandr snatched him in the middle of his shift, guarding the town's healer. But a beautiful voice keeps caressing his mind, demanding Fen do things he doesn't even understand. All he knows is the flawless wolf he can't shake makes the voice go away. Fen has his sights on a gorgeous unmat-

1

ed wolf, Kyrie. He has no clue if he can win Kyrie or if he should bother while his head is such a mess. It's possible his time as a prisoner broke his mind. He has a bad feeling the hallucinations are real. Fen has an even worse suspicion that truth might break him.

Kyrie has... secrets, to say the least. He also has a problem with occasionally dropping dead. He's working on both. The last thing he needs is a sexy Scottish vamp in his life. That doesn't mean he doesn't want him. Kyrie simply needs a miracle if he hopes to keep him. Surely, that's not too much to ask, especially when he has an open line straight to the Gods. Well, one God, and it's destroying his life.

Unwanted is the fifth book in Charity Parkerson's Devilish series where vampires, Weres, demons, gods, and all manner of the supernatural live together beneath the noses of humankind. These books are best when read in order.

Chapter One

THE CITY LIGHTS TWINKLED across the sky, blotting out the stars. All it had taken was a simple thought. Fen had gone from his home deep in the secluded mountains of Wulfe, Washington to the bustling heart of Seattle. Fen had been born and raised in the forests of Scotland. He was more accustomed to the silence. So, he couldn't explain why he loved the city so much. Everything was loud and busy. The lights were too bright, and life moved at a clipped pace. There was all the entertainment he lacked back in Wulfe, where he had been assigned to protect Frost. It was a lofty position. Frost was important. Not only was he the town's Druid healer, but he was also special in ways even Frost didn't know yet. Fen had been a personal guard to the Scottish vampire king for more years than he could recall before he had been called to serve in the U.S. His position in Scotland had been a dangerous job, but familiar. Still, when he had been called by his Goddess, Celeste, to protect Frost, he hadn't hesitated. It was an honor to serve, but sometimes he wished he could settle here where no one knew his past.

Fen was restless in a town where everyone knew everyone. Joy had vanished from his life overnight after being abducted in a feud between gods. He didn't recall a thing thanks to Celeste wiping his memory. The effects lingered nonetheless. Food tasted disgusting. He wasn't one of those vampires who had tired of eating and stopped. Fen still wanted to savor life. He just didn't know how anymore. His life had dimmed and everyone knew it in Wulfe.

That was why he had come to the city. There was a restaurant he wanted to try, and he was out from beneath a suffocating microscope. He was certain if he tried the right dish, things would turn around. Maybe his life could go back to normal. As he pulled open the door of the small Italian restaurant, the most delicious scents he ever encountered slapped him in the face. A waiter turned. Their gazes met. A smile exploded across Fen's face. Just seeing Kyrie always made him beam. Kyrie was a young Arctic wolf from Wulfe. The world was truly a small place.

Yellow eyes, too bright to be human, headed his way. Obviously. Fen knew the eyes were connected to Kyrie's body, but they were the only thing he saw as the space between lessened.

"Hey." The breathless greeting pulled Fen from the edge of saying something dumb about Kyrie not hiding his animal side.

Fen's smile wouldn't dim. "Hey. I didn't know you worked here."

Kyrie's smile stayed intact too. "Yeah. For a few years, actually. I've never seen you come in."

"This is my first visit. I'm still on the hunt for something that doesn't taste horrible after my..." They were in public. He didn't know what to say.

"Since Monnie," Kyrie finished for him.

Fen's smile fell. He snapped to attention. Fen hadn't heard anyone use that name for Jörmungandr except in his weird dreams that wouldn't stop. "Why did you call him that?"

Someone waved for Kyrie's attention.

Kyrie made an oops face. "Sorry. I have to get back to work. Sit anywhere you like. I get off in fifteen and I'll join you."

Fen wanted to laugh at the audacity, but he couldn't say he didn't want Kyrie to join him. He picked a table and sat to wait. Kyrie's gaze kept sliding his way. Fen couldn't stop staring. He wondered if he made Kyrie uncomfortable. A certain intensity vibrated from him and Fen couldn't rein it in.

"You have to tell me where you get your contacts. They're amazing."

Fen hid a smile when the question floated his way from a nearby table.

"Sure thing. I'm at the end of my shift, but I'll write the website on your check."

Fen wondered if the guy had set up an affiliate account at some costume contacts site. Surely he got asked that a lot. Kyrie disappeared into the kitchen. A good ten minutes passed before he reappeared, carrying a tray of food.

He paused at the table with the contacts inquiry. "I wrote the web address, as promised. You can pay upfront whenever you're ready. No rush."

After a few more pleasantries, Kyrie headed his way with the tray. Fen expected him to drop it at a different table. Instead, he sat with the food at Fen's table.

"I haven't ordered anything yet."

Kyrie's eyes danced with laughter. "I know, but I'm the expert here. Trust me, you'll like this. It's not on the menu. I made it especially for you."

Fen's eyebrows rose. "You cooked this?"

Kyrie smiled. "Aye," he said, mocking Fen's thick Scottish accent.

For the first time in a long time, Fen didn't think about anything but the moment. Kyrie was breathtaking. That had nothing to do with looks, even though the guy was arguably a bonnie lad. He shone brightly from the inside. Kyrie was sunshine in a bottle. Fen couldn't stop staring at the way his eyes lit with mischief and humor.

"Take a bite," Kyrie urged, obviously impatient with Fen's hesitation. Little did Kyrie know Fen had forgotten there was food.

He scooped a bite of some sort of ravioli or tortellini looking stuff into his mouth. Something indescribable melted on his tongue. His insides sang. While Fen's heightened senses picked apart every flavor, they came together to create the perfect combination. For the first time in forever, Fen was famished and knew he would walk away satisfied.

"Well?" Kyrie looked as if he held his breath. There was something else about his expression too. Fen fought the urge to scrape the thoughts from his mind. Wolves were lesser beings than vampires. He could easily pluck anything he wanted from Kyrie's head. For once, Fen didn't want that. He wanted to be surprised by what came next.

"This is the best thing I've ever put in my mouth. How did you do this? It's like you're magical or something."

Kyrie made a dismissive gesture. "My best friend and I used to stay up cooking all night, trying to find combinations of food he could eat without gagging. He was a vampire. I lived with his family," Kyrie added, as if that wasn't unusual, before moving on. "His mom used to stay so angry with us for destroying her kitchen. Then I started cooking for them

12

too and she didn't care anymore about the mess."

Fen was fascinated as hell. "Do you have nae kin?"

Kyrie lifted his shoulder in a half shrug. "My mom died in childbirth, which is pretty common among our species. My dad didn't stick around. I was sent to Wulfe to be raised by my mom's pack. They passed me from home to home until I was twelve. That's when they called me grown and said I could choose who I wanted to live with full time. I chose Neo's family. They were the only constant in my life. They were the steadiest I felt. What about you? Do you have any family?"

Except for the fact that Kyrie wasn't eating, this felt like a date. Kyrie picked up a breadstick and started picking it apart before popping bits into his mouth. If he didn't know better, Fen might've thought Kyrie read his mind and challenged him to deny it was a date.

Fen bit back a smile. Kyrie was cheeky. Fen liked him. "Aye. I have a brother in Scotland. My brothers and father were on the battlefield with me when we were cut down. Only my older brother and I survived long enough to be turned. My mam died from old age a long time ago."

"How old were you when you were turned? You look to be in your early twenties."

Fen nodded as he chewed. He took a drink of the water Kyrie had brought him before answering. "Twenty-five. How old are you?" He took another bite.

"Twenty-one."

Fen nearly spit out his food. While Fen had been turned at twenty-five, he had been that age for many a century. He had never felt so old...or perverted, honestly. This wolf was a child.

Kyrie's eyes flashed dangerously. "I'm not a child."

"Did you just read my mind?"

Kyrie chuckled. It was a soft sound that caused goosebumps to rise on Fen's skin. "Your thoughts were in your eyes. Enjoy your meal. It's on me."

Kyrie stood.

Fen panicked a bit. "I did nae mean to offend. You just made me feel verra old for a moment."

Kyrie held his stare. It was the most serious Fen had seen him. "I'm not offended. It's a long drive home. I know when I've outstayed my welcome and I can't be home in a flash the way you can. Like I said, enjoy your meal. I'm glad I could help."

Before Fen could think of a way to stop Kyrie from leaving, Kyrie was out the door. All Fen could do was stare at the space where he had been. If Fen was good at one thing, he excelled at ruining dates. That truly sucked. When Celeste had asked him to move to Wulfe, he had secretly hoped he would find his fated mate. After all, Celeste paired the souls. Surely she wouldn't continue asking him to serve for the rest of eternity without honoring him with a mate. Life was incredibly lonely after hundreds of years of meaningless encounters. He craved a soft place to land. Each day that passed without that blessing got harder than the last. Between the emptiness, the dreams, and the voices in his head, Fen didn't know how much he had left to give. Maybe it was time to walk into the fire.

Bring me the wolf.

Like conjuring the devil, the words brushed his brain. He had no idea where the demand came from or what the words meant. It was possible he had gone around the bend. And fuck, he had completely forgotten to ask how

Kyrie knew the name Monnie. Everything was a disaster. That tracked.

In complete silence, Kyrie made the trip home. He didn't even bother turning on the radio. His social battery and tolerance for sound had been completely drained. Some wolves didn't get to be young. Kyrie topped that list. He was exhausted and lonely. Tired of rejection. Lights passed by, hypnotizing Kyrie. He zoned out, driving on autopilot. Every-thing blurred. Life took on an edge of surreality. Kyrie blinked. His car sat in the driveway of his duplex. Kyrie had zero memory of how he had gotten home. That was scary. He needed to get some sleep.

Wolves howled in the woods at the edge of his backyard. Kyrie's skin itched. He wanted to set his wolf free and run. Just keep running until he dropped. Wher-ever he landed, he would start a new life there. There was nothing for him in Wulfe. He was different. Everyone knew it. No one wanted to claim a child everyone knew would put them in dan-ger. All it took was one look at Kyrie's eyes to see he wasn't full wolf. There was more in his blood. Something pow-erful. Dangerous.

As Kyrie stumbled through the front door into the darkness, everything looked as bright as day to him. He tossed his apron full of tips on the couch and headed for the kitchen. Kyrie was terrible about remembering to drink or eat. That half a breadstick he had shared with Fen was all he had eaten in probably two days. He supposed he'd had water at some point in the day. While it was fairly affordable to live in Wulfe, especially with a pack discount, Kyrie stayed too exhausted to cook for himself and too broke to eat takeout all the time. He was one hundred percent sick of the food from work. Kyrie simply stood in front of the open refrigerator door and spaced out. Was he even hungry? His hands tingled with numbness and his vision darkened around the edges. An invisible weight sat on his chest, slowly suffocating him. Everything spun and then went black.

Ambrosia filled his nose, overwhelming his system. He felt like he floated on a cloud. Fingertips softly stroked his cheek. Kyrie nuzzled closer to the touch. Goddess, he missed affection. Soft lips brushed his, drawing a moan from Kyrie.

"So exhausted. I should let you sleep."

Kyrie's chest ached at the idea of losing the invisible arms surrounding him, even though they didn't love him. If he woke, his house would be empty. His life would still be totally devoid of comfort. Only when the darkness swallowed him did he find solace.

"Oh, beautiful. I miss you too. Sleep. Dream."

Kyrie wanted to obey. Something gnawed at him, keeping him from sinking deeper into the abyss. Kyrie fought the hot tears that pressed against his eyes. His chest felt like it might cave. None of this was real except the emotional pain. Each time the other side pulled him toward destiny, the less Kyrie craved life. He craved genuine peace.

"Damn, Kyrie. Are you okay? Do I need to call Frost? Your car and front door were standing wide open. Fuck it. I'm getting Frost."

Kyrie blinked. The shadow of a man hovering over him took shape. Still, Kyrie couldn't fully see.

The mystery figure vanished.

Kyrie struggled to sit. His refrigerator stood open with Kyrie's body blocking it from closing. "Goddamn. My electric bill is going to be through the roof this month." A startled cry escaped him as two figures popped into his kitchen from nowhere.

Frost immediately dropped to his knees next to Kyrie. He looked like he had been pulled from bed. "Tell me what happened."

Kyrie's hands rose and fell. He worried if he opened his mouth, he'd cry.

"I found him unconscious."

Kyrie's gaze slid Fen's way. His mind cleared a little more by the second. Fen looked panicked. Kyrie tried to focus. His head spun.

Frost checked his pulse, and a small light hit Kyrie's eyes. Life didn't come into full focus until Frost set his hand on Kyrie's chest. Warmth spread from the spot Frost touched. Frost's pretty green gaze moved over Kyrie's face.

"When was the last time you ate?"

"He had half a breadstick with me at dinner."

Thankfully, Frost didn't react to the news they'd had dinner together. Of course, people ate together all the time.

Frost completely cut Kyrie from the conversation. "Did he drink anything?"

Fen seemed to think about it before slowly shaking his head. "Not that I recall."

Frost checked Kyrie's pulse again. "If you were human, I'd have you on an IV right now. Unfortunately, with the rate you heal, I'll only risk an IV under extreme circumstances. Still, I'm on the fence. Do you think you could give me a urine sample?"

Kyrie tiredly shook his head. He wasn't even sure he wouldn't faint again.

"That's what I thought. I need to take some blood. Your pallor and vitals have me worried about your kidneys. Obviously, you're dangerously dehydrated."

Before Kyrie saw it coming, not that his mind was clear enough to anticipate anything, Fen grabbed Kyrie's wrist and bit. The world vanished again, but oddly, he still heard the rapid beating of his heart.

"Can you keep control of his mind? Anything I give him for pain will burn through too fast to help. Keep him unconscious if you can."

Rapid-fire phrases flew around him. Kyrie really couldn't pinpoint who spoke or what happened. Everything felt out of his control. Nothing felt real. Then everything was gone again.

Chapter Two

THE NONSTOP PACING PROBABLY drove Frost and Gemini crazy. If so, the couple never said a word. Technically, Fen was on duty. He was still at Frost's house and could protect Frost. But Kyrie was there too, being kept as a patient, and he still hadn't woken. Fen couldn't help but blame himself. If he hadn't insulted Kyrie, Kyrie would never have run out before eating something and hopefully drinking something as well. After all, they had found him in front of a near empty refrigerator. Was he trying to kill himself? Did he have an eating disorder? Was he too poor to buy food? Surely, that last one wasn't the problem. Kyrie was a wolf. He could hunt. Kyrie didn't need the grocery store. Maybe that was why his fridge had been empty. Possibly it had nothing to do with anything. Maybe he had just gotten busy and forgotten his body needed sustenance. A voice in the back of his head screamed that he knew that was a lie. Wolves didn't get this bad from one day of neglect. Fen was so fucking confused. He wanted to talk to Kyrie. Drill him for answers. Assuage his guilt. But fuck, Twenty-one? He had known Kyrie was young. There was no way Fen could have foreseen that number. It didn't really matter. He had just been caught off guard. Fen understood why he had upset Kyrie. He got the impression Kyrie hadn't gotten to be young.

As if Frost had been musing over Kyrie too, he just started talking like they had been having a conversation about Kyrie all morning. "It's baffling. There's nothing physically wrong with him. His kidney function was terrible, but it immediately rebounded after a bag of fluids. I don't understand why he won't wake up."

Gemini jumped in. "You know supernatural creatures have different physical systems. Maybe you need to look closer at his bloodwork with that in mind."

Frost shook his head. "That was my first thought." He shook his head again while staring into space. "It's almost funny. If I didn't know he was a wolf, I'd say he's—"

"Half something else."

Everyone's gaze flew to the mouth of the hallway. Kyrie stood, looking closed. Fen couldn't pinpoint exactly what it was about Kyrie's expression. His face was clear of any emotion, but his eyes burned with rage and pain.

Frost was on his feet. "How are you feeling? Let me check your vitals."

Kyrie took a step back before Frost reached him. "That's not necessary. Thank you for coming to my rescue. Just let me know how much I owe you." Kyrie's gaze never moved Fen's way. A defensive coldness chilled the air.

Frost drew up short, seemingly as confused as Fen. "I don't think you should leave yet. We need to make sure this doesn't happen again."

"Why?" Kyrie held Frost's stare. Fury rolled off him. "So you can share my business with everyone? Did you hesitate even a second before putting my existence in jeopardy? I think I'll pass."

Frost's shoulders fell.

Fen's heart went out to him. Frost had been tossed into their world with no warning or training on how his new community's bodies worked. He was learning as he went.

Frost's defeat hung heavily in the room. "You're right. I apologize. You don't owe me anything. I work for Celeste. If you want to file a complaint, and I don't blame you if you do, just pray it to her, I guess. I don't know how any of this shit works." Frost's ran a hand over his face as if tired as hell. He sounded more downtrodden with each word.

Kyrie's cold stance seemed to deflate. "There's no need for all that. Like I said, I appreciate your help." His voice softened. "For future reference, it's pointless to intercede. It's not possible for me to die." He headed for the door.

Fen shot a desperate look Frost's way.

Frost made a shooing motion. "I'll be fine."

That was all the permission Fen needed. Things had been quiet for a long time and Frost had plenty of eyes on him. In truth, Fen wasn't sure why they were still there. Lucifer meant Frost no harm. In fact, the dark god kept Frost safe. The rest of them were useless by comparison, but their orders hadn't been updated, so they just kept showing up to guard duty.

Fen stayed hot on Kyrie's heels. "How do you plan to get home?"

Kyrie didn't slow. "I might look like a child to you, but I can find my house."

Fen pinched the spot between his eyes. Kyrie was obviously still angry.

"*Och*, I know you're nae a bairn. I'm nae attracted to children."

Kyrie froze. He slowly turned. His expression remained closed, but at least he wasn't running. "What did you just say to me?"

Fen was no coward. If he had been better with words last night, they wouldn't be in this mess. "I realized after you left last night, you're the reason the food tasted good. It had nothing to do with some special concoction of ingredients. The meal was only enjoyable because I spent it with you." Fen found the hint of discomfort he hadn't thought he would feel by being brave. "Not that your cooking is nae impressive, but the way your eyes danced with laughter distracted me so I could eat. The moment you left, everything dulled again, and I couldn't finish."

"Is that why you showed up last night? So I could help you eat?"

Damn. Kyrie was determined to stay mad. "I came so I could regain the happiness your company brings to me."

He saw the fight leave Kyrie. In the absence of his fury, Kyrie looked ten steps beyond exhausted. Fen didn't know what thoughts went through Kyrie's head. Whatever they were, Fen would do whatever it took to bring back the smiles. Maybe he was too old for Kyrie, but Fen couldn't be the reason Kyrie lost his shine. That would be a disservice to the world.

Gemini felt the defeat inside Frost. He shut Gemini out, making Gemini want to punch things. Frost was always so damn determined to carry things alone. As his mate, his inability to share the load hurt Gemini's chest. They were a team, but most of the time, Frost still lived like an island.

Frost headed down the hall.

Gemini shot to his feet and followed.

Frost fell facedown across the bed. His emotions hit Gemini full force. Frost

wanted to quit. He felt like a failure and tired as hell. Gemini climbed
onto the mattress and scooped Frost
into his arms. He settled down, using
Frost as a blanket. Frost cuddled closer, as if searching for Gemini's heartbeat to comfort himself. These were the
only moments when Gemini thought he
might not be failing as a mate.

*I'm the only failure in this room. You're
the most amazing mate in the world.*

Oops. Frost had been in his head. Gemini rubbed Frost's back, doing all he could
to soothe him. "Talk it through with
me."

He felt Frost shrug. "I don't know what
I'm doing. Celeste should've never chosen me for this. When I was a real doctor, I never would've violated a patient's

privacy by openly discussing their case like that."

"First off," Gemini cut in. "You're still a real doctor. Second, Kyrie is a good kid. He probably already feels guilty. Third, Celeste chose you because you absolutely have what it takes for this job. You're brilliant. You just need someone safe to bounce ideas around with. I'm your mate. Talk to me like I'm your partner because I am. What do you need to make you feel better equipped?"

He heard the thoughts flitting through Frost's head before he said a word. "I need study material. When I get patients, sometimes I know exactly what to do—like Celeste floods my head with info. But if I knew more about all the various anatomies, I'd feel more confident in my decisions. I'd feel like I have some sort of control because I've put the work in."

Gemini got it, but still. "You have put the work in. I think you just overthink everything and undermine your abilities. Like, what would you do if Kyrie was human and had a mystery illness?"

"I'd look closer at his bloodwork and run more tests," Frost answered without hesitation.

"Exactly." Gemini kissed the top of his head. "So let's go do that. Just say every thought you have on his blood out loud. Maybe hearing yourself will trigger something. It's possible I might know some random fact that pertains to Weres."

"Okay." Frost sat up. He flashed Gemini a sad-looking smile. "Let's do this."

Gemini rolled upward and wrapped himself around Frost's back like he planned to go for a piggyback ride. "Not yet." He kissed the side of Frost's neck before licking and sucking. The way Frost's breathing changed had Gemini poking at his thoughts. Frost threw some images at Gemini that had Gemini whimpering.

If you plan to make me miserable while I work, you're going down with me.

Gemini chuckled against Frost's skin. *Oh, I'll go down. But not before you use that genius mind and take another look at that blood again.*

Frost released a put-upon sigh. "Fine." Without warning, Frost stood holding on to Gemini and headed for the makeshift surgicenter King Jonathan had created for Frost.

Gemini panicked a little. He was a Were leopard. His body weighed more than a human's. Yet Frost made the stroll like Gemini weighed nothing, with Gemini clinging to him like a monkey.

You know, this is kind of hot.

Frost glanced over his shoulder and smirked.

Damn, there was so much about Frost that changed every day with the magic in his druid blood growing. One thing that never changed was the way Gemini felt. Love, attraction, and need muted everything else in his life. Frost was the oxygen he breathed.

When they reached the lab, Frost let Gemini down. Gemini sat in the chair next to Frost's chosen seat. He watched Frost work. He took a small drop of blood from a tube and put it on a slide before slipping it beneath his microscope. Gemini stared at Frost's sexy profile while Frost inspected his sample under the light.

After a minute, he sat back. "Huh. I wish I had blood samples from other creatures to compare. I know Kyrie doesn't want me to know his business. But if I don't know his exact species, how am I supposed to help?"

"I'm a Were. Take a sample of my blood and see how it compares."

Frost brightened. "Are you serious?"

He looked so damn hopeful, Gemini couldn't say no. Also, it had been his suggestion. "Of course. You're my mate. I want to help."

"Okay." He sat forward again, grabbing a lancet and an alcohol pad.

Gemini chuckled as Frost scrubbed the tip of Gemini's index finger before quickly sticking it. "I'm immortal."

"I know, but you're able to get sick. If not, I wouldn't be needed in this field. I won't risk infection."

He supposed that was true.

Frost smeared a drop of Gemini's blood across a different slide. He gave Gemini a cotton ball for his finger as if it hadn't already healed. Then he went to work again. Frost studied his blood for a while, going as far as to switch slides several times. He straightened and flipped on a monitor connected to the high-tech microscope.

"I want you to see this so someone will know I'm not crazy." With the click of a button, the blood sample appeared on the screen. "This is your blood. It's honestly not that different from human blood, except it's like quadruple the cells, and if you watch, the cells keep multiplying. It's as if they are still trying to repair themselves even though they no longer have a use."

Gemini nodded. He followed Frost's line of thinking. So far, it sounded like simple stuff.

Frost switched slides.

Gemini sat forward. He was pretty sure he completely stopped blinking. "What the..."

"Exactly." Frost sounded relieved he wasn't overreacting. "Have you ever seen anything like this?"

Gemini shook his head. He was transfixed. "There are some red blood cells, but it looks like he has glitter in between."

"Or actual light."

Gemini's gaze snapped to Frost's face. "Is it light?"

Frost shrugged. "It's possible."

He was all the way invested. Gemini understood why Frost had been shocked into talking about Kyrie's case without permission. "Use your blood. Let's see the difference."

Frost shrugged. "I'm just human."

Sometimes, he aggravated Gemini. Gemini huffed. "You're not just human, and I thought you wanted samples of all varieties to compare. You're Druid. How would that affect your blood?"

Looking more than a little curious, Frost grabbed a new lancet. "Good point. I haven't had any bloodwork done since I became your mate." He didn't wipe his finger before stabbing it.

Gemini huffed again. "Why did I need alcohol, and you don't?"

Frost shrugged, but he flashed Gemini a smile, softening the way he blew off Gemini's concerns. "I'm immortal." Frost laughed when Gemini rolled his eyes. He quickly did his thing and changed out slides. He didn't switch views, so he could inspect it alone first. Gemini got to see the results in real time. They both froze. Frost's blood was a near identical match to Kyrie's. The only difference was Frost's cells didn't multiply, trying to heal themselves.

"What the fuck?"

Gemini nodded, understanding the sentiment. "Is he half Druid?"

"No."

Their heads whipped toward the door. Kyrie leaned against the frame and watched. He didn't sound angry as he had before, but neither did he look pleased.

Frost looked crestfallen again. "I'm sorry. I just wanted to find out how I can help you. This falls under patient-doctor confidentiality. I swear I'm just working on your case."

Kyrie's bright yellow eyes flickered Gemini's way before returning to Frost. "I suppose your mate would know everything you know, no matter what. As is his right. So I can't really be mad about him helping, which is also his place. I came back to apologize for how I reacted earlier."

"No. You had every right to be angry," Frost said, cutting him off. "I was fully in the wrong."

Kyrie drew a deep breath, looking exactly like he fought a battle with himself. He released the air in an audible sigh. "Your job here in Wulfe is to keep us healthy. I'm sure you feel like you can't help if you don't know someone's history. I'm trying to keep you safe here. Sometimes not knowing is the best protection."

Gemini got it. He knew Frost did too. It was there in his mind. There was something bigger happening. It had been building since Frost got to town. Whatever secret Kyrie held in his blood could bring terror to their town, and goddess knew what to Kyrie. Unfortunately, considering Frost's blood looked similar, what did that mean for him? Nothing good, he feared.

Frost spoke on their behalf. "I'll destroy all the samples."

A sweet smile touched Kyrie's lips. He looked so young and tired. Gemini's heart went out to him. He didn't know what burden Kyrie carried, but Gemini wasn't blind to how Kyrie had been made an outcast in this town, even by his pack.

Kyrie straightened from the door frame. He wobbled a little, as if every ounce of energy suddenly slipped from him. "I think I need to—" He hit the floor hard. Just totally dropped. His body landed at an angle that had Gemini certain Kyrie was dead even as he shot to his feet to help.

"Holy shit." He raced to Kyrie's side. Frost landed on his knees at the same time as Gemini. They immediately went to work.

Fen came crashing into view. "What happened?"

Frost met Gemini's stare. "He doesn't have a pulse."

Gemini's mind locked up, failing him at the time of crisis. Kyrie had really dropped dead, and he had no clue what to do. What the hell was in that blood sample?

Chapter Three

Icy cold water engulfed him. Anticipation hit Kyrie before the dread set in. More and more often, Kyrie found himself pulled into the heavenly sea. When the first dream came, Kyrie had woken alone and confused. Everything had felt so weird—like he didn't belong in the real world anymore. His entire existence had turned colder. Each smile got harder to fake. Kyrie found himself trying to get back to his peace. Sometimes, Kyrie wondered if he had started down a slippery slope he couldn't return from. It seemed as if he diminished a little more every day. One day, maybe he wouldn't wake up—forever dreaming.

His feet gently landed in the sand. A warm, tropical breeze washed over him. Peace settled into Kyrie's soul, stealing away any rational thoughts. Maybe he didn't want to go back. Perhaps he had finally come to the point where he could leave the world behind no matter what the destination. The smell of coconut teased his nose. Kyrie closed his eyes. He loved that scent. It reminded him of a certain brand of body oil people used at the pool to get the perfect golden tan. These dreams were as close as he would ever get to a vacation. Life was expensive, and Kyrie was a little too used to human conveniences to live full time as a wolf. He didn't get into the whole letting nature provide, leaving worldly goods behind. Kyrie loved worldly goods—like air conditioning and winter coats. He was not an outdoor wolf, but he was in love with the ocean. One day, it would be his.

As the delicious scent engulfed him, so too did a set of familiar arms. Kyrie found himself lured backward against a very solid chest. He was cozy—like sinking into his favorite sleeping position. It really was too bad he didn't know when that affection would turn to pain and fury.

Warm lips skimmed the shell of his ear.

Kyrie smiled. "Didn't I just see you?"

He felt Monnie shrug. "You're addicted to me. I can't help it if you keep fighting your way back to me, but I'm okay with that."

Of course, he was unbothered. It wasn't his life that had been upended by this half-life. Once upon a time, he hadn't minded. Lately, everything had turned against him. Real life was still empty. That was his only constant.

"You're not alone. It looks like Fen has taken an interest."

A small smile passed over his lips at just the sound of Fen's name. As much as he hated to admit it, Fen gave him a reason to hope. But he needed to remember where he was and hide his thoughts. "I'm pretty sure he doesn't actually want to be interested."

A soft chuckle rumbled against his neck. "Fen might be a vampire, but he's still a man. Not even the gods can fight that." Monnie's hand slipped down Kyrie's body, shaping every line and curve. "It's impossible for him to see this, combine it with the sunshine you bring into every room, and still stand firm in his black and white sense of morality."

Kyrie leaned his head back, fully relaxing against Monnie's perfect body. Sometimes, he still wished nothing had changed between them. When he spoke, his voice wouldn't work beyond a whisper. "I know things will turn out how fate decides, but..."

Monnie gently spun Kyrie. As always, Kyrie stopped breathing the instant he saw heaven swirling in Monnie's unnatural blue eyes. They didn't only look like the sky. They were the sky. His nearly white blond hair was the clouds. Everything about him was as flawless as any god. Irresistible. Monnie's mouth quirked. "I need you to stop thinking about my body if you want me to be serious."

Longing raced through Kyrie's blood. Maybe if he seduced Monnie... "I'm tired of being serious."

Monnie didn't back down. "We don't have much longer. The clock is ticking, but I very much want everything you do." He held Kyrie's stare while he pulled the bandana loose that Kyrie kept around his wrist at work. It was all fake. He had to remember it wasn't real. Monnie slowly brought Kyrie's wrist to his mouth and kissed it while never breaking eye contact. An unsteady breath stuttered from Kyrie's lungs. "You have to focus on Fen. It's time." Monnie whispered the words between the sweet kisses he placed on Kyrie's wrist. He looked so turned on and in love. Kyrie swallowed hard, trying to fight the devastated tears. None of this existed. Monnie was right. Kyrie had to focus on reality. It was time.

Fen sat in the corner and stared at Kyrie until his vision blurred. Then he blinked and started the process all over again. He watched tears flow from Kyrie's eyes. Fen desperately wanted to know why Kyrie cried in his sleep. Maybe he was in physical pain from this mystery illness. Fen had tried several times to poke at Kyrie's mind. There was nothing but an impenetrable wall. Fen had never been so scared and confused. Honestly, it was strange. He should be able to see Kyrie's every thought. Fen had no clue how Kyrie unconsciously blocked him. Maybe he was nearer to not returning from this state than anyone realized. That was a heartbreaking thought.

Fen had lived several lifetimes. He had watched people he loved more than anything grow old and die or never even see middle age. Fen didn't know Kyrie that well. For some unexplainable reason, he couldn't focus on anything other than Kyrie's health right now. Maybe it was the mystery of it. Not only was Kyrie immortal, but he was also young and seemingly healthy. It made no sense for Kyrie to be in this position.

Kyrie's eyes suddenly blinked open. His gaze landed on Fen as if he knew exactly where he sat and that he would be there. They held each other's stare. The exchange felt strangely pivotal, as if some silent and important message passed between them. Fen didn't know what happened, but he knew he didn't want this to stop. A delicious scent tickled his nose. It was a hell of a time for his hormones to spike. What in the hell was actually wrong with him when it came to Kyrie?

"You're awake. That's awesome." Frost looked relieved as hell as he breezed inside the room. He focused on Fen. "I'm sorry. I have to ask you to step away for a bit while I speak with my patient."

Fen got it. Frost had already broken patient privacy once, and Kyrie had been furious. He wouldn't risk that twice. Frost needed to look as professional as possible now.

Fen dipped his chin, acknowledging the request. He focused on Kyrie. "I'll be around if you need me."

A sweet smile passed over Kyrie's lips. "Okay."

Fen left, closing the door behind him. His heightened hearing caught the first few words.

"I'm thrilled to see you awake. As much as I hate to press the issue, it's gone beyond critical to know your parentage. The only way—"

Gemini appeared in the mouth of the hallway. "Hey. I thought I heard someone moving around. Come join me outside. It's a nice night and I have beer."

Fen wasn't blind, nor was he dumb. Gemini had Frost's back on the privacy issue. Fen pasted on a smile and headed Gemini's way. "Sounds great." He let Gemini lead him outside. As they stepped out, he was greeted by more people than expected. Leif and Audor were there. Since both men were Frost's guards, he had known they were like-ly there somewhere. He hadn't real-ized Audor's husband, and the town's pack leader, Waylon, was also there, along with Frost's best friend and her husband, Jacen and Deidra. The fairies were another staple in Frost's home. The only genuine surprise was Stone. Stone had guarded the Scottish vam-pire king at Fen's side for years and had been assigned to join Fen in America. He was always all smiles and naughty behavior. The guy was impossible to hate.

Fen nodded at everyone as he headed for the empty seat at Stone's side. "Hey. Where have you been hiding?"

A bright smile lit Stone's face. "You know me, getting to know the town."

AKA, trying out as many beds as possible.

Fen shook his head. "Someone will find a way to kill you someday."

Stone winked. "Not when you're good."

He wanted to be irritated with Stone's flippancy, but there was just something about the guy. Before Fen could think of a way to respond, Stone took control of the conversation.

"How's your boy?"

Fen opened his mouth to say Kyrie wasn't his. The thought was gone as quickly as it formed. "Honestly. I don't know. Frost is in with him now. Hopefully, he'll figure this out."

Stone nodded along. "Frost was sent here for a purpose, just as we were. Kyrie will pull through."

Frost stepped outside and headed Fen's way.

Fen went on alert.

Thankfully, Frost didn't make him ask. He motioned toward the house. "Kyrie wants to go home. You should be the one to take him."

Fen tried to decipher Frost's tone without luck. There was something there. Frost seemed worried and distracted.

Still, Fen stood. "Of course."

Before Fen made it two steps. Frost touched his arm, stopping him.

His eyes seemed slightly desperate. "Will you stay with him? I always have Gemini's protection. You should focus on this. I'm certain Celeste would understand."

Since Frost seemed to have a direct line to their goddess, he dipped his chin. "Nae harm will come to him."

Frost's shoulders visibly relaxed. "Thank you."

Fen didn't bother saying Frost didn't need to thank him. They both already knew. For whatever reason, Kyrie was his responsibility, and Fen never shirked his duties. Fen headed for Kyrie's room. The same amazing scent overwhelmed him as soon as he reached the mouth of the hallway. Fen didn't know how he knew it was Kyrie, but he did. He smelled like the sea and freedom. Tropical flowers and a fruity drink on the beach. Coconuts. Fen's mouth watered. His stomach clenched with hunger. He froze. It had been a while since he'd fed. He should do that before going home with Kyrie. The last thing he wanted was to be in a position of Kyrie smelling like the perfect meal while he starved.

Bring me my wolf.

Fen shook his head. The hallucinations were back. For fuck's sake. Maybe they really were fueled by the strange hunger he had suffered since his abduction. He would let Kyrie know he needed a moment to feed before they left.

Kyrie appeared in the hallway. The scent got stronger.

Fen felt his fangs grow.

Something passed over Kyrie's features. "Your hunger pains are sitting on my chest." He motioned Fen closer.

Fen's feet moved a few steps. He stopped. His mind went fuzzy until Fen shook it off again. "Nae. I'll be fine. You need your strength."

Kyrie simply held his stare, leaving Fen to fight with himself. He didn't press Fen. Fen was the one who couldn't stop thinking about Kyrie's blood. He had sipped from him that one tiny time, testing his blood for dehydration. Fen swore he could already taste him. His pulse pounded in his ears. No. Kyrie's pulse beat at his eardrums. He moved closer, like his body was on autopilot. Fen smelled the unique blood that pumped through Kyrie's delectable body. He tasted like paradise, and Fen knew it.

Kyrie held his hand out, wrist up, tempting Fen closer.

Fen gently took his offered arm. He stared down at the tiny blue lines just beneath the skin's surface. The sound of rushing blood got even louder. It was all Fen could hear. Two tiny white scars caught and held Fen's attention. He brushed his thumb over the marks. A sharp pain stabbed him through the chest unexpectedly.

Fen lifted his gaze. "You have a mate."

Kyrie held his stare with something desperate in his eyes. "I do."

An image flashed through Fen's mind. He saw himself barely sinking his fangs into Kyrie's wrist for half a second. "Dear Goddess. It's me."

Chapter Four

THOUGHTS RACED THROUGH KYRIE'S head so fast, he couldn't hang on to them. Technically, in the bare minimum way, Fen had claimed him. Kyrie hadn't done the same. He didn't know how Fen would ultimately react. Kyrie wasn't sure Fen knew how to react either. It was like he was paralyzed. Kyrie didn't think he even blinked. They stood awkwardly in Frost's hallway while Fen did whatever he was doing.

Kyrie had felt terrible for a while now. He wanted to go home and rest before he had to go to work and kill himself while already half dead. His nerves snapped. "It's fine if you don't want me. I know you think I'm too young and it's barely a scar. Who knows if it even fully took? I don't have to claim you. We can just pretend—"

Fen lunged forward. His mouth cut off Kyrie's nervous, racing speech. As Fen's tongue curled around his, the air changed. Kyrie knew Fen had transported him home simply by the familiar smells surrounding them. Fen held him lovingly while exploring Kyrie's mouth. Kyrie almost felt treasured, but he still didn't think Fen wanted this. He knew next to nothing about mates. No one really bothered to explain it to him. He felt pretty fucking desperate to crawl under

Fen's skin so they could live as one person. That probably wasn't normal.

Fen chuckled against Kyrie's lips. "Your thoughts are hilariously all over the place."

Kyrie didn't know if he should huff or cry. He didn't think people were supposed to laugh under these circumstances.

Fen held Kyrie's face between his hands and pressed his forehead against Kyrie's. They held each other's stare. Fen's eyes were even more beautiful up close. "I'm laughing because I'm happy. Also, a little because I'm not crazy."

That one stumped him. "What made you think you're crazy?"

"Lots of things." Fen sounded very matter of fact. "How I felt at dinner the other night. Why the scent of your blood makes me ravenous." He stole another quick kiss. "Why you taste so damn good."

Kyrie's heart turned over in his chest.

Fen didn't stop. "How it felt when you dropped." Fen's expression turned to pain. "It was suddenly like part of me died. The pain was excruciating. You can nae do that to me again. I thought I'd go insane."

Kyrie reached up and held on to Fen's wrist where Fen still cupped Kyrie's face. He didn't want Fen to disappear. "I don't know what's happening to me, but I don't plan on going anywhere. But I also have no clue what to do next, and it feels like someone is crushing my chest."

Fen swept Kyrie from his feet and headed for the bedroom like he had been there a million times before. "I want you to claim me, but I don't know if you're strong enough right now. I don't even know how a Were reacts to vampire blood. Waylon and Audor are the first case ever of this type of mixed mating, as far as I know. We're evenly going into this blind." He gently placed Kyrie on the bed and then climbed in beside him. Fen tucked the covers around them, ensuring Kyrie was as warm as possible. "There."

Kyrie took a chance and cuddled against Fen's huge body.

Fen dragged him even closer.

Kyrie hid a smile against Fen's chest. He had literally no clue where this was headed, but Fen hadn't left. That was something. The desperation to tear into Fen's skin and make him his was nearly crippling. Unfortunately, his weak body cared nothing about Kyrie's emotions or desires. Weakness owned him.

Fen's brain and body were all over the place. Kyrie was his mate. All these

years with nothing. Maybe he had always been fated to have a wolf mate,
but it had been impossible until recently.
Fen fought a snort. Kyrie hadn't been
alive that long. Fen had to get past that
shit. Really, he already was. He just
needed to tell himself anything right
now to stop his urge to rip into Kyrie's
throat and give him the mark he deserved. Matters weren't helped by Kyrie
not claiming him. Kyrie had literally died earlier. This wasn't the time.
He needed to regain his strength. Kyrie
would tolerate his arms around him.
That was one right he couldn't aban-
don—illness or no.

Fen's mind betrayed him by making up
excuses for a blood exchange. Maybe
Fen's blood was exactly what Kyrie
needed. Vampire blood was stronger

than wolf blood. Fen forced the idea away. He still didn't know Kyrie's heritage. For all he knew, Fen's blood could make him worse. The taste of Kyrie's blood that he had gotten was so fast and small; he couldn't even recall the taste, much less decipher its makeup. They were mates, though. Technically, Fen could just reach into Kyrie's mind and find the information needed. Fen immediately discarded the idea. Kyrie could probably feel him poking around in there. If he wasn't careful and came off as controlling, Kyrie might never claim him. Fen already wanted to claw at his skin like an addict needing a fix. Having a mate and staying unclaimed was physically painful, especially since Fen had claimed Kyrie. He felt adrift and out of control. Kyrie hadn't even mentioned claiming him, had he? Fuck. Fen had been slightly out of his head since seeing those faint fang marks on Kyrie's wrist. He had given up hope too long ago to recall. Now he had all these growing desperations. Finding his other half had him fucked up. The impatience was thick. That didn't matter, though. A good mate would cater to Kyrie's health first, and that was exactly what he planned to do.

Even though Fen held Kyrie, it wasn't enough. He hoped he didn't feel this lost and unwanted forever. What if Kyrie didn't want an old vamp? He hadn't enjoyed any real freedom yet. Hell, he might be a virgin for all Fen knew. Oh, Goddess. Was he a virgin? Fuck it. Fen tried gently slipping into Kyrie's mind. A smile exploded across Fen's face. All his fears vanished.

Kyrie slept and dreams filled his head. All Fen could do was linger and watch. He was too captivated to move. Kyrie was in wolf form, on his back in the snow, with paws in the air like he tried to catch the sunlight. The dream was too peaceful for Fen to look away.

I know you're there. Come play with me.

It took Fen a second to realize Kyrie spoke to him. Kyrie had to turn his head and focus on Fen for him to see the truth. *Only if it's okay for me to disturb your peace.*

Actually, I find your company very soothing.

Fen sat in the snow next to Kyrie. Without thinking, he ran his fingers through Kyrie's white fur. It was thick and fluffy.

I'm an Artic wolf. This is my happy place, but I also love the sun. Oh, and the beach. And the sea. The water is so much fun, but not so much when I'm a wolf. The fur gets kind of heavy in the ocean.

Fen loved the purity of Kyrie's thoughts. He was nothing like the warriors that had surrounded Fen his entire life. The quiet that settled into Fen's soul was comforting as hell. Kyrie was very much a soft place to land.

You probably wish you had some of my fur on your butt right about now.

A loud bark of laughter burst from Fen. His face hurt from how big his smile had grown. Just the way Kyrie held his head with his tongue hanging out the side of his mouth was too cute. It was the most adorable of wolfy smiles. Fen felt good on the inside. "My plaid keeps me warm. Plus, it's nae likely to bother me too much in a dream. I could probably just picture having a hairy arse."

Kyrie turned human. The transformation happened in a blink. The happiness had gone from his expression. He wasn't laughing. "Do you think you can't hurt in a dream?"

"Holy fuck." Fen reacted on total instinct. He scooped the very nude Kyrie from the ground and used as much of his body as he could to protect Kyrie from the cold.

Kyrie's serious expression never wavered. His gaze moved over Fen, as if searching for something only he knew. "Do you want this? Are you mad you got stuck with me? I saw your face when I told you my age. I'm not who you wanted. What's he like?"

Fen was confused as fuck. He felt the heavy sadness inside Kyrie. Kyrie truly believed Fen wouldn't have chosen him if given the chance. That there was someone else out there Fen longed to have.

I can only hear the thoughts you give me, but I can feel your disappointment.

As the thought brushed Fen's mind, he remembered a crucial detail. Fen had claimed Kyrie. He saw and felt everything Kyrie did. Fen could reassure himself with a single dip into Kyrie's mind. Kyrie hadn't claimed him. He couldn't do the same. Fen kept forgetting that, and he was hurting Kyrie. "Wake up. Take my blood. I want you to have the ability to run through my mind and see how blessed I feel."

Kyrie slowly shook his head. Deep sadness filled every corner inside him and the pressure of his misery nearly choked Fen. "Something isn't right. Something feels forced. If I claim you and feel a single ounce of rejection from you." Kyrie shook his head again. "Being unwanted by you might be the thing that finally stops this heart for good. I feel weak all the time anymore. Weary. I don't know what's wrong with me, but I know I can't carry the weight of your discontent. That's too much. Having a mate for all eternity who would've chosen anyone but me, you can't ask that of me."

Fen was beyond devastated. He was in Kyrie's head. Kyrie believed every word he said with his entire being. Fen's reaction to his age had been a blow at just the right time. The perfect storm of a day. He couldn't see what happened, but he felt every ounce of emotion attached. Kyrie was defeated inside. Fen had just found his mate, and already he failed him.

Chapter Five

WHEN KYRIE OPENED HIS eyes, he wasn't surprised to see Fen staring at him. On their sides, face to face, life turned intimate. It felt like everything else vanished, leaving them in a bubble that belonged only to them—like they couldn't be disturbed. Fen had claimed him. By accident or not, Kyrie felt so much, he thought he might explode. It was unnatural for only one of them to be tied to the other. Maybe that was all the heavy feelings crushing him were all about. Kyrie didn't know how much of what he felt was real. Hope was a damnable thing.

That pesky emotion didn't give a shit about common sense. Kyrie couldn't stop crashing himself against the rocks, hoping just one love would stick.

He couldn't have stopped himself from moving if he tried. Fen's eyes silently begged Kyrie to help him. Kyrie stopped thinking about himself and what he couldn't survive. His mate hurt, and it was Kyrie's job to soothe him... no matter how temporary life might be.

"Please?"

The quiet plea broke Kyrie. He couldn't listen to Fen beg. Mates went deeper than regular relationships. It was a life bond he couldn't walk away from, no matter how much he feared the future. It would be the same for Fen.

Kyrie urged Fen onto his back before straddling his body. He slowly lowered his head and swiped his lips across Fen's. It wasn't enough. Kyrie deepened their kiss. Fen matched him, staying at Kyrie's pace. Kyrie appreciated that more than Fen could ever know. He supposed that wasn't true now. Fen could see inside his head anytime he liked and know exactly how much Kyrie needed his patience.

Kyrie kissed a path from Fen's mouth to his neck. The dark thoughts that kept undermining him sneaked in as he kissed the spot inches below Fen's ear. Maybe he should choose a less visible spot. Fen might not want a mated mark where anyone could see at first glance. Then again, Fen was a vampire. Maybe he wouldn't scar at all. It was possible he could just pretend they weren't a set. Did Audor have a mark? Damn it. He couldn't recall.

A shaky-sounding breath escaped Fen as Kyrie licked the spot he kissed. Fen writhed beneath him. He grabbed the back of Kyrie's head and gently held him in place. "Yes. Right there. I want it."

With that sexy tone, Kyrie would give him anything. He bit. His fangs took over, tearing into Fen's throat. Blood filled his mouth. Kyrie swallowed. The orgasm that hit him had Kyrie praying the feeling never ended. Something invisible tugged at his chest. He felt the laces stitching them together as one. He was too overwhelmed to be terrified.

The moment Kyrie removed his fangs, Fen healed. Kyrie watched the marks form with lust and love clouding his vision. He had a mark. Everyone would know Fen was off limits.

"I need that too."

Kyrie's back hit the bed before he could decipher Fen's words. A starved vampire was on him. Kyrie's clothes were ripped away. "I need the world to know you belong to me and only me." His gaze met Kyrie's. Fen's stare looked crazed. "Don't worry. I'd never let you hurt."

With only that as his warning, Fen vanished into thin air. Before Kyrie could form a thought to wonder what happened, Fen was back. "What—"

Fen impaled him.

Kyrie's mouth opened in a silent scream. He hadn't been prepared. Even though, logically, he knew Fen was in his head blocking the pain, and he had obviously disappeared and coated himself in lube, Kyrie still hadn't expected the sudden intrusion.

Then Fen's fangs sank into Kyrie's throat, and nothing mattered. In fact, he was absolutely thrilled to have Fen inside him when the second orgasm hit. It was a totally different experience with Fen enjoying it too. He felt the blood leave his body as Fen drank. The sensation was muted by the way his soul sang and the sounds Fen made as he joined Kyrie over the edge. He hadn't known what to expect when he claimed Fen. There was no way Kyrie could have envisioned this... not under the circumstances.

Fen's thoughts barged inside Kyrie's head and set up shop. Kyrie felt everything Fen did, and sunlight burned away all the darkness inside him. Not only did Fen want him, but he also wanted this entire package. Kyrie was his miracle. Fen had tried resigning himself to never having his second half to roam the earth with him for all of eternity. Kyrie saw that night at the restaurant through Fen's eyes. While he had been caught off guard by Kyrie's age, the knowledge didn't stop the attraction. He adored Kyrie's company. This union mattered to him more than anything.

Tears filled Kyrie's eyes as Fen licked Kyrie's neck, sealing the wound faster than Kyrie would have healed on his own. Kyrie felt the pride that roared through Fen as he stared at the scar that proved Kyrie was his. Tears spilled back into Kyrie's hair. He wasn't alone. Kyrie had a mate. Thank every deity. Maybe now the dreams would stop.

Fen knew he had been too rough. Claiming his mate had broken him down to his most primal state. Now Kyrie cried and Fen felt like an ass. He just couldn't seem to do anything right lately. Honestly, his head had been all over the place since he came to Wulfe. It was very possible he had known deep inside his mate was here, but that didn't excuse anything.

Stop.

Fen startled a little. It was a new sensation, having anyone in his head. Under normal circumstances, he was too old to read. "Sorry." He kissed Kyrie's forehead. "My mind is a bit of a mess. That's not on you."

Kyrie didn't respond.

Fen tried checking his thoughts.

Kyrie had him shut out.

Not only was Fen old and strong as hell, but Kyrie was his other half. He shouldn't have the ability to keep Fen out. "Talk to me, please? Your silence weighs on my chest."

"Sorry. I'm not trying to punish you. I'm just used to keeping everyone out."

"Why do you do that? What are you afraid people will see?" Fen had to know. There was something growing larger inside him, driving a forceful need to protect. To his bones, Fen knew Kyrie had something big going on in his life. They were mates. Whatever happened to Kyrie happened to him.

Kyrie twisted his fingers and chewed his bottom lip. Fuck, he was beautiful. Unexpectedly, a smile exploded across Kyrie's face. "Your thoughts are pretty. I don't think I've ever felt this at peace."

"You don't look like you're at peace." Fen hadn't meant for the words to burst out quite so forcefully, but damn. "Until you smiled just then, you looked ready to run."

"Maybe I'm just a nervous, skittish person."

Fen snorted.

Kyrie's smile grew bigger. "Yeah, I know. I'm hard work."

A laugh burst from Fen. "You're feisty." Kyrie laughed, so Fen kept going. "Do you prefer spicy?"

Kyrie's smile didn't dim as he dropped his bomb. "My dad is Freyr."

"He's still out here making kids?" Fen couldn't say why that was what popped

out, or why he had sounded so disbe-
lieving. It was just honestly his first
thought.

"Well, he is the god of fertility."

Reality sank in a little deeper. "Wow."
Fen cleared his throat. He honestly had
no idea how to feel. "That's definitely
a reason to keep people out." The more
he thought about it, the more sense the
confession made. That explained why
Kyrie said he couldn't die. He definitely couldn't. It also explained why Fen
hadn't suffered from any hunger pains
since the moment he sampled Kyrie's
blood to check his health until the moment he faced Kyrie in Frost's hallway.
He had known there was something familiar about it. Fen had his own secret. He knew why nothing tasted good

anymore. Jörmungandr had addicted him to his blood and continually wiped the memory from Fen. That shit had stopped working for some reason. He clearly recalled Monnie forcing him to drink from him in his dreams. Fen hadn't wanted to believe those dreams were real. Now he knew he wasn't crazy. They were real.

Kyrie's gaze moved over his face, studying him. He looked serious and loving, and like everything Fen had ever wanted. "The dream world exists. It's just as real as we are now. You have to be careful there. It's run by sprites commanded by Monnie. Celeste is your deity, keeping you safe, but you belong to me now. I don't know what that means for you. Maybe he could pull you in where no one can rescue you."

Confusion overwhelmed Fen. Things were sounding way bigger than he had considered so far. "I belong to you as your other half or..."

"I'm sorry I didn't tell you before I claimed you. You're the mate of a demigod now. No one rules you, except maybe me. But that's just mate stuff—like me killing you if you touch anyone else. That sort of thing. Unfortunately, you're still no competition against a god and we're alone in the world." Kyrie's gaze dropped. He looked so sad, but he brushed feet with Fen beneath the covers. "At least, I am. You probably have lots of people to call if you need help."

"You have me." The statement sounded every bit as forceful as he was on this matter. Kyrie was his. No one would ever hurt him. Fen was a warrior, and maybe that was why Celeste had chosen this amazing blessing for him. He could and would protect Kyrie with his life. The gods would have to see him dead if they wanted his other half. Fen was greedy like that.

Chapter Six

WHEN WAYLON, THE WULFE pack leader, had been blessed with a vampire mate, there had been a slight pushback from a few of the town's residents. There had been some rumblings from the older generations and some of the hardcore young traditionalist. They hadn't wanted a mixed breed pairing. Before Audor and Waylon, there had never been a case of a wolf ending up with a vampire. Well, there had been rumors of a three-person mating of a human who had been blessed with both a werewolf and a vampire as mates.

Apparently, they were special in some way. Otherwise, everyone knew the two species couldn't share the same soul. Odin had forbidden it. It seemed times were changing. The gods were mixing things up, and—apparently—Fen was *messy*, messy. The first thing he suggested for the day was breakfast at the diner. Everyone ate there or hung out for gossip sessions throughout the day. Kyrie felt the eyes on them.

When he couldn't take it any longer, Kyrie tore his eyes from the menu that hadn't changed in his entire life. He focused on Fen. *What thoughts are being tossed our way?* Kyrie knew Fen could read everyone in the room. Kyrie couldn't use his powers like that. Plus, he just liked making Fen feel special.

Fen's beautiful green gaze skimmed the room. "I wonder if everything will still taste nasty to me." Fen said the words aloud while speaking with Kyrie personally at the same time. *Most are happy for us. There're a few young wolves who are jealous. Only one is thinking a ton of bigoted shit.*

"Order what used to be your favorite and find out." *Which one?*

Grey Canis.

Kyrie rolled his eyes. *Fuck that old bastard. Apparently, when I was brought to town, he took one look at my eyes and told my pack to toss me on the fire.*

"What the actual fuck?" *I'm curious what Freyr would've done.*

Kyrie chuckled. *He's the god of fertility. Not the god of parenting. I've never even set eyes on him.*

Fen reached across the table for Kyrie's hand.

Kyrie didn't hesitate to take it. Peace settled inside him as their fingers linked. He didn't need anyone else.

"Damn right."

Kyrie chuckled again. This was the best thing that ever happened to him. He refused to believe anything else.

"Are you two ready to order?"

Kyrie flashed their server, Sarah, a smile. "You know I'm boring."

Sarah smiled as she wrote Kyrie's order. Kyrie truly had lived a monotonous life. He always ordered the same thing. At least for breakfast, anyhow. He didn't like that many breakfast foods.

"I'll have what he's having."

Sarah nodded. "Do you two need anything else, or are you good for now?"

I thought you planned to get your favorite as a test.

"We're good." Fen focused on Kyrie the moment they were alone. "Funny story. Your regular is my favorite."

Kyrie shook his head, but he couldn't contain his smile. He couldn't have been given a sexier blessing. Kyrie was on top of the world.

Fen smirked. *Keep up those thoughts. We won't get to eat.*

Whoops. "What did you want to do after this?"

Fen looked slightly uncomfortable. "We have so much to figure out."

Kyrie nodded. "I know. This came from nowhere. You probably feel like I'm a complete stranger."

"Do you feel that way?"

Fen's question caught him slightly off guard. He hadn't been prepared to have the question tossed back his way. "No. I know you."

"Same. Since that night I offered to do a full moon run with you, I've been a little obsessed." Fen looked embarrassed, but he kept going. "You have no idea how much I regret not going, especially since I was totally useless by staying behind to comfort Leif. He disappeared before I could speak to him."

"Speaking of which." Kyrie lowered his voice. "Did you ever find out what that was all about?" They had been enjoying a nice bonfire and barbeque at Frost's house when a large Werebear had shown up. Leif had taken one look at the guy, turned, and ran for the hills.

Fen sipped his drink before responding. "Yeah. It seems Leif was head over ass in love with the Werebear who crashed the party that night. They used to be in a decades' long relationship, before the reality of never getting to be true mates finally destroyed them. Now, pairings like ours are happening. It seems the bear came as soon as the rumors hit his pack. Leif has no desire to see him. Apparently, things did nae end well."

Kyrie's chest hurt. "That's so sad. I hate how much that story isn't rare. Lots of people have gotten their hearts ripped out for the same reason."

Fen nodded. "I know a few others as well."

Their food arrived. Sarah arranged their plates. "Can I get you anything else?"

Kyrie flashed her a smile. "We're good for now. Thank you." When he looked Fen's way, Fen took a cautious bite.

Oh my, goddess. Thank all the gods.

A smile exploded across Kyrie's face. "I take it you're cured."

Fen nodded as he shoveled food in his mouth.

Kyrie had known he would be back to normal. Sadness chose that moment to claw at his guts. Kyrie shielded Fen from the pain. Of course, Fen was better. It was all part of the plan. He wished like hell he was stronger. But Kyrie had never been meant for happiness, and that was enough to defeat anyone. Kyrie understood now that was exactly why Monnie had chosen him. He was the weakest link.

Their feet kept brushing beneath the table. Fen had never been happier in his life. Each time he locked eyes with Kyrie, all the feelings overtook him. Finding a fated mate was something no one could prepare for or describe. He wanted to go straight to Kyrie's place, pack all his stuff, and have him moved in by night-fall. There was still this tiny part of him that felt like he was being over the top. He didn't know if Kyrie wanted the same things. He had been a little scared to pick through Kyrie's thoughts and find out for himself. It was possible Kyrie wanted to go slower. There was no chill in relationships like theirs, but Fen was prepared—sort of—to do whatever Kyrie needed. Well, he could wait for any furniture movement. No way would Kyrie sleep away from him again. That was asking too much, especially with the weird dropping dead thing.

Fen didn't start the conversation until they got back to Kyrie's place. "What's going on with the—"

"Just let me grab some things and we can head to your place," Kyrie said at the same time.

Fen blinked. He hadn't expected that. "Aye."

Kyrie headed for the bedroom.

Fen followed. "How can I help?"

Kyrie didn't respond until he opened his closet door. "I don't know. How much is too much?" He glanced behind him. "I know you're probably not ready to have me living with you or anything, but I also don't really want to sleep apart."

Fen didn't even think. He snatched up the closest piece of furniture. It might be daytime, so he wasn't at full strength, but he was still strong enough to get Kyrie out of here in no time.

A loud laugh burst from Kyrie. He bent at the waist and laughed even louder—like he couldn't stop and couldn't catch his breath.

Happiness overtook everything, even as confusion filled him.

Kyrie waved a hand as if asking him to wait while he got himself under control. He swiped at his eyes as he straightened.

The emotions Fen saw staring back at him had Fen ready to move mountains.

Kyrie finally found his voice. "None of the furniture is mine. I'm renting the place fully furnished."

Fen gently put the dresser back. "*Och*. Sorry. I guess that looked a little extreme."

Kyrie's smile never dimmed. Good humor danced in his eyes. "Honestly, that's exactly what I needed. I haven't done anything except second-guess my every choice since the day we met." Thankfully, Kyrie didn't make him ask what he meant. "I've berated myself a hundred times for telling you that you should stay and talk to Leif. Then that night at the restaurant, it felt like the greatest date, even though I was working, yet I walked away the moment I got my feelings the tiniest bit hurt. Still, you came for me when I needed help. My dumb ass still resisted. I don't know what I'm doing."

Fen heard in Kyrie's thoughts how scattered he felt. "We're learning together. You've had little to nae family to guide you. I've only ever been a warrior. But I think we're doing great, and I believe in us." Fen had moved closer during his speech until he stood toe to toe with Kyrie. His beautiful yellow eyes seemed to glow brighter than usual. Fen was helpless against the call of Kyrie's soul. He tucked a strand of Kyrie's hair behind his ear. Fen lowered his head. Kyrie met him halfway. What Fen meant to be a sweet kiss exploded into an inferno the second their lips touched. The world could fall around them, and Fen wouldn't know. One second, they stood in the doorway of Kyrie's closet. The next, Kyrie was beneath him.

When Fen popped open the button on Kyrie's jeans, Kyrie seemed to find an ounce of sense. He turned his head, panting, as Fen moved his attention to Kyrie's neck. "The sun is up. You zapped home last night. I'm fairly certain you didn't bring that lube with you."

Fen moved south, unconcerned. "Don't worry. I have different plans for you."

Kyrie's shirt didn't stand a chance against Fen's strength. He easily tore it open so he could lick Kyrie's nipples.

Kyrie buried his fingers in Fen's hair and writhed beneath him. "My skin is on fire."

"I've got everything you need." He massaged Kyrie's erection through his jeans.

Kyrie's hips left the bed, blatantly seeking more. A whimper escaped him.

Fen wouldn't let his mate suffer. Kyrie would always get everything he wanted. Fen went straight for the pleasure. In an instant, he had Kyrie's erection out and in his mouth. He felt everything Kyrie did. Fen was all the way in Kyrie's head, savoring every lick and sucking pull. His hips moved of their own volition. He humped the bed with zero shame. Fen forgot everything except the way they felt together. Fen had never wanted anything in life more than the exact mate he had been given. Now he needed Kyrie to scream his name.

Kyrie held Fen's hair and took what he wanted. They were one. Kyrie had to know how much Fen loved the abuse... and the way Kyrie wasn't shy about his desires. Eternity was a long time. This would only get better, and Fen wasn't sure he would survive it. He already felt like the building orgasm would tear him to pieces.

Kyrie's body tensed.

Fen's did too. He already knew Kyrie's orgasm would be his. He practically tasted the intensity. The insanity.

Kyrie exploded with a loud cry.

Fen coated the inside of his jeans with cum, reminding him he hadn't removed a single piece of clothing. As Kyrie rode out his orgasm on Fen's tongue, Fen fought for his life. The emotions choked him. Too many feelings pressed on him at once. This was really his. His body hummed in a way it never had before. Pleasure overtook his entire being. He shook from the way his cock wouldn't stop spitting cum. He didn't stop licking Kyrie's dick until there wasn't a single twitch left to pull from him.

Ragged breathing filled the air. Words clogged Fen's throat. He had no clue how much of what he needed to say would make him sound like a lunatic. He had no choice.

Fen took a deep breath. "I—" A loud banging on the front door cut his words short. They froze. Fen focused his mind on the door. It was Waylon on the other side. He didn't stop banging.

Fen stared down the line of his body. With his heightened senses, he smelled the cum all over them. There was no way a powerful pack leader like Waylon wouldn't smell them too.

"It's okay." Kyrie gently untangled himself and quickly stripped away what was left of his clothing. "Hold on! I'm coming!"

Fen buried his face against the mattress and bit back his laughter at Kyrie's choice of words to yell at the door.

In no time, Kyrie cleaned his skin with the discarded remnants of his shirt. He pulled on a robe before heading for the door. "Hey, Waylon. What's up?"

Fen heard every word as if he, too, stood in the doorway.

"I saw Fen's truck in the driveway. Leif didn't show up for his shift."

Fen jumped from the bed, completely forgetting his chaotic state. He was at Kyrie's side in an instant. "What's happened?"

There was no hiding the mess that he was, but Waylon never acknowledged his cum-soaked jeans or even dropped his gaze below eye level.

Waylon was in full sheriff's mode. "I don't know yet. Audor worked the early morning shift. Leif was supposed to come in by noon. He didn't show. I know you're in your honeymoon stage right now, but Audor can't leave until someone relieves him and someone needs to find Leif."

"I'll head to Frost's place. Fen should go after Leif. He's better versed in vampire matters."

Waylon glanced between them at Kyrie's offer. It was beyond obvious he didn't think Kyrie could protect Frost. Little did he know there was no one stronger in Wulfe.

Fen chimed in. "Kyrie can handle the job." He held Waylon's stare, silently demanding Waylon take the hint without an explanation.

Waylon looked between them again. His gaze finally stopped at holding Kyrie's stare. Fen knew what he saw. Glowing yellow eyes with no true wolf traits. He gave a sharp nod. "I appreciate your help."

Like that, their day was sidetracked. For all the reasons in the world, Fen wasn't surprised. Nothing ever went his way.

Chapter Seven

THE VIBE AT FROST'S house was weird. It was like everyone waited for the other shoe to drop on a completely unknown situation. No one really spoke. Kyrie felt several odd looks tossed his way. He stayed in wolf form and kept his thoughts hidden. Maybe he was only paranoid, but he swore every nearby vampire poked at his brain. Kyrie kept his nose to the air and avoided eye contact.

At the edge of the forest, Kyrie caught the scent of a bear. Kyrie glanced around, making sure no one watched before he slipped between the trees. The bear didn't try to hide. In fact, he sat still, openly waiting for Kyrie. He was a big guy. His scent seemed familiar.

Kyrie turned human. "Have we met?"

The bear turned into a man Kyrie was certain he had seen before. "Aspen," he said, as if reminding Kyrie of a name he should know. "We crossed paths briefly at Frost's a while back."

The memory hit. Aspen had crashed one of Frost's barbecues. It had been the same night Fen had offered to run under the full moon with him. Kyrie dipped his chin. "Kyrie."

Aspen's sweet brown gaze moved over Kyrie's face. "You're the wolf mated to a vampire."

This was the one in love with Leif. Kyrie's heart went out to him. "I am. A pairing that seems to be growing around here."

Pain crossed Aspen's features and stabbed Kyrie in the chest. "Not for everyone, I guess." He cleared his throat and moved on before Kyrie could think of anything comforting to say. "Is there any news on Leif? It's not like him to shirk his duties. He's always taken pride in his service to his goddess."

Kyrie wouldn't know. He hadn't given much thought to the vampires who invaded the town since Frost's arrival. "I've not heard anything yet. How can

I help? How can I make this easier on you?"

A sweet smile passed over Aspen's features. He was adorable. "My feelings don't matter. I just need to know he's safe."

Kyrie's heart went out to Aspen. Life really didn't give two shits about anyone's feelings. It just crushed and crushed until there was nothing left of the soul. "Like I said, I haven't gotten any updates, but I literally just got here like fifteen minutes ago. I can keep you posted, if you'd like. Just let me know how to get ahold of you."

Aspen's gaze moved over Kyrie's shoulder before meeting his stare again. "I'll find you."

Kyrie smelled Frost heading their way.

In an instant, Aspen was back to being a bear and ambling away.

Sadness filled Kyrie as he turned to greet Frost.

There was a deep line between Frost's eyebrows. "Is Aspen okay?"

Kyrie lifted his hands and dropped them again. He never knew how to help anyone. Sometimes, he got the feeling Frost felt the same way. "I don't imagine so. It's obvious he really loves Leif. I could feel it just standing close to him. How are you?"

Frost sighed. "I'm fine, but it seems like everyone else isn't. How are you feeling? Have there been any more incidents?"

"None." Of course, Kyrie wasn't surprised by that. Monnie had plans for him here. That didn't really mean anything, though. Time moved differently in the heavens. Monnie could snatch him at any time. Kyrie's breath stayed held for just that.

"Strange."

Kyrie nodded along, trying to look as stumped as Frost.

Frost brightened. "Nice mating mark there, by the way. I think you two caught everyone by surprise."

Kyrie chuckled. "Yeah. Us too."

Frost's smile didn't dim. "I'll bet."

An adorable, fluffy snow leopard appeared. A low angry-sounding warning purr filled the air.

Kyrie rolled his eyes and turned back into a wolf. *Nothing worse than a jealous mate.*

Frost's eyebrows shot up. *I can hear you. Can you hear me?*

Of course. I can hear whoever I want. You can too.

"What?" Frost practically screeched the question.

Kyrie shook his head. *I think it's time you asked Celeste a few tough questions.* Kyrie focused on Gemini. *Good to see you, as always. I should get back to work.* Kyrie walked away, leaving behind the mess he had likely made. This was a town filled with too many secrets. Maybe it was time some of them broke loose.

Stone appeared like a wraith at his side. "Feeling especially messy today, are we?"

Kyrie chuckled. *Maybe so. It's past due, don't you think?*

"Aye. Things have been a wee boring as of late. I'm a vampire of action." He waggled his eyebrows at Kyrie.

A snort escaped Kyrie. *Seeing a lot of action in Wulfe?*

Stone tilted his head, looking thoughtful as they strolled the perimeter together. "Admittedly, no. No offense, but this town is a mite dull. Thankfully, I can zap to wherever I want. There are lots of fun places around the world."

I'll have to take your word for it since I've never been anywhere. Since I was technically born in Sweden, I suppose I've been there, but I don't remember it.

"*Och.* That's unacceptable. If you ever want to go on an adventure, come find me. I'm a lot of fun." The sexual energy that dripped from Stone's every word definitely worked on everyone he met. Kyrie didn't doubt that for a moment, but Kyrie wasn't having it. *Pardon you, sir. I'm a mated wolf.*

Stone stopped and turned Kyrie's way. He stared into Kyrie's eyes in a way that wasn't at all comfortable. "Are you, though?" Without waiting for Kyrie to swallow past the lump in his throat and give a response, Stone walked away, whistling.

Kyrie sat staring at nothing while seeing way too much. He felt everything slipping from him already—the way it always did. People in Wulfe were starting to see through him. He had stayed too long.

The first stop Fen made was Leif's place. He figured Waylon had checked there before coming to Fen. However, Fen was willing to do something the town sheriff was not. He broke in. While Fen knew he could probably wait until dark and just drop in, he worried they didn't have time for that. What if no one had come for him when he had been abducted? Fen wouldn't pussyfoot around while something horrible could be underway.

The small house in the middle of town was totally silent. Nothing looked trashed or anything like that. There didn't seem to have been any type of struggle. Fen walked through each room before searching for any hint of where Leif might have gone. He found a note on the fridge.

Audor,

I imagine you'll be the only one who looks for me. Sorry for skipping out like this without a goodbye. I suppose you heard about Fen and Kyrie.

Fen sat. It hurt his heart that it looked as if he was part of the problem.

Between your finding your mate, and now Fen also being blessed with what I prayed so hard for all those decades, I just can't do this any longer. Aspen is here, and it's just too hard. I hate that I sound like an asshole right now, but I know I've been acting like one too. You have no idea how much that bothers me. You're my best friend. Unfortunately, the anger and bitterness have beaten me. The jealousy doesn't care that you're like a brother to me. Centuries of service to Celeste has meant nothing. All these years of being filled with pride at knowing I honored my goddess have absolutely been a waste. She obviously doesn't feel I'm worthy, and I can't keep kneeling at her feet any longer. So, I guess it's time to do something else, free of this chore. Please let Frost know it's not personal. I have to do this for me. I have to cut this tie before the anger buckles me. It's been an honor to be your friend. Long may you live in peace and happiness.

Leif.

Fen stared at the note, seeing nothing. He understood. Fen couldn't say he hadn't experienced the same thoughts in his centuries of service. More so, of late. He had been on the verge of losing hope too. Maybe that was why Kyrie still felt too good to be true. In his heart, he knew there was a slight disconnect he kept hidden. He kept waiting for the other shoe to drop. In no way was he more deserving than Leif. It felt odd as hell to go from the deepest despair to having the biggest blessing bestowed upon an immortal: a permanent love to walk with until the end of time. Time truly was unending when a person was alone. He didn't think Leif could be blamed for his decision. Not that he knew how Celeste reacted to having a warrior turn their back on her. He very much knew what she did to people who abused the powers given to them. Fen had been one of the old king's personal guards. He had been there to witness her wrath. King Adair had abused his position in some of the worst ways. When Celeste had snapped her fingers, turning him to naught but dust, all Fen had felt was relief. Fen didn't want to see the same happen to Leif. They had only worked together a short spell. Really no time at all in their eternal lives. But from what he had seen, Leif was a good man whose only fault had been falling deeply in love with a bear he would never have. It was just sad for everyone involved.

Audor strolled into the kitchen. His expression was completely devoid of emotion. Still, Fen felt the pain he kept hidden. Leif and Audor had been a team since their Viking days. This would be a real blow to him.

"So he's gone, then."

It hadn't been a question. Audor already knew. Fen handed him the letter. "This was on the fridge."

Just as Fen had done, after only a few short lines, he sat at the kitchen table. His gaze moved over the paper in a way that screamed he read the words a dozen times. Finally, Audor dropped the paper and sat back in his seat. "Well."

"Aye." Fen honestly didn't know what to say. A part of him felt like he should apologize, but he wouldn't. As much as Leif had earned the same blessing Fen had been given, Fen also deserved the amazing mate Celeste had passed to him. Life wasn't a pie to be divided. He didn't know why some people got chosen and others didn't. Sometimes he wondered if even Celeste knew. Maybe even Celeste was a victim of the whims of the Fates, pulling everyone's strings. Things just were what they were.

"Tell me how I can help." That was all Fen could offer. It wasn't as if they could or would give up the unheard of pairing they had gotten.

Audor shook his head. "Tell me how and why this happened to us and not him."

"I can't." All Fen had was honesty. "As much as I know I deserve a mate, I don't know why I was given a wolf. Why now? Why us? I don't understand what's happening. I don't know what's changed in the heavens. But absolutely it's nae fucking fair to Leif. I saw the way he looked at Aspen when he came to town."

Audor nodded. "When they were together, their love was almost cloying." Audor's ice blue stare bored into him. "So too was the fear of watching one or the other wake up in love with someone else, all because they stood no chance. It was like walking on eggshells, holding your breath. When they parted ways, it was almost a relief, as horrible as it is to say."

"Nae as terrible as it would've been to watch one see the other with their true mate."

"Exactly. That would've been soul crushing, and I get it. When I fell in love with Waylon, I felt the same. He kept bringing up how we were temporary. Any chance of forever with us was impossible. I finally had to walk away to save myself. We weren't together that long by any sort of comparison. I can't even imagine spending decades building a life only to have to finally come to grips with reality. Now that reality is all skewed. He's right to be angry."

"Aye."

They held each other's stare. A silent message passed between them. This was bad, and there was nothing anyone could do to stop whatever came next.

Chapter Eight

FEN CAME HOME TO find Kyrie sitting on his doorstep. He looked every bit as defeated as Fen felt. This was supposed to be their time, yet they were forced to carry the guilt of being chosen for some bigger-than-them plan or whatever. Fen didn't say a word. He simply scooped Kyrie from the stoop and carried him inside. Kyrie never looked away from him. There was no need to speak. They equally understood how rare and precious they were—and that was the problem. Countless beings had been in their shoes since the beginning of time. Yet for some unknown reason, they had been brought together as nearly strangers and with Kyrie so young to boot. They saw the unfairness and felt the jealousy pressing in on them. Life should be so beautiful for them now. The circumstances made a picture-perfect life feel like no more than a dream. Maybe they should run too.

"Don't even think that. It'd be a slap in Celeste's face if you walked away now."

Fen had known Kyrie would hear those thoughts. Maybe part of him wanted Kyrie to take the decision from him.

He felt the heavy sadness as it filled Kyrie. Fen sat on the couch, keeping Kyrie on his lap and in his arms. He stared at Kyrie, waiting for him to say what pain he hid.

Kyrie stared at his lap. When he finally spoke, it was barely a whisper. "Maybe it's a slap in my face how much you regret this."

It was like getting stabbed in the heart. The absolute heartbreak of Kyrie's one hundred percent belief that Fen regretted him was too much. Kyrie's pain choked him. He had been so unwanted and rejected his entire life. Fen saw and felt it all. Kyrie's suffering took down the wall Fen had seen in Kyrie's mind, and it was there. Him, being a literal toddler, listening to adults—his family—discuss who would get stuck with him: the abomination. They hadn't known he was part god. All they had seen was a mixed-breed puppy. His entire childhood, one adult right after the other, simply packed him up one day and sent him to be someone else's burden. Then he saw the overwhelming happiness that came when he met Neo. The vampire family had been thrilled to have a second son. Kyrie loved them with all his heart. It hit Fen. The only time Kyrie had mentioned Neo, he had said his best friend was a vampire. Was. Past tense. Kyrie had gotten his first job. All it had taken was three nights of him working, leaving them alone, and the three had been slaughtered by some unknown entity. Kyrie might not know who had done this terrible thing, but he knew it was his fault. They had known his secret. It wasn't like a teenaged wolf could hide his thoughts from a pack of vampires. To his soul, Kyrie knew their murder was his fault. Someone sought him. So Kyrie had kept to himself for the most part, never sharing his secret again. Now he had opened himself to Fen, only to see everything slipping away and rejecting him all over again, except that wasn't happening. Fen wasn't going anywhere and he sure as hell didn't regret a damn thing about them.

Fen kissed Kyrie's forehead and let him see the hundreds of years he lived without Kyrie. The endless battles and the worst possible king until a few years back. All the nights of coming home to nothing but silence. Then he showed Kyrie the moment he saw that faint scar on Kyrie's wrist. Everything inside him had shifted at that moment. His long existence had suddenly been worth every bit of his wait because he had been given the most beautiful man alive who also made him smile like he hadn't in centuries. Fen had been so moved, he had fought tears that night.

He heard Kyrie swallow, as if it was painful. "I'm sorry. I get that it seems like I don't trust in us. It's just I—"

Fen cut him off. He couldn't listen to Kyrie berate himself to bleed for Fen. Fen didn't need that. "Stop. I understand. In our world, I know it's different and everything is supposed to immediately be one hundred percent perfect. You're supposed to just know nothing will ever go wrong because this is your other half. But when life has never given you a damn thing except what can go wrong, it's hard as hell to believe there's anything out there that won't eventually bring you nothing but pain."

By the end of his speech, Kyrie stared at him like he saw the miracle they were. He looked as if he trusted Fen and finally recognized exactly how much Fen wanted this. This was all Fen craved since the moment he realized Kyrie was his. When he thought of running away, it was because this was all he needed now. Fen was exhausted with duty. Getting abducted had finally broken something inside him. He just wanted to sit in peace. Kyrie was that tranquility he sought.

"Can we just walk away for a night? I'm overthinking everything."

A smile tugged at the corners of Fen's mouth at the question. That was exactly what they needed. "The sun is going down."

"It's a full moon."

Kyrie looked hopeful and Fen wanted all the same things. "Let's go for a run."

The smile that exploded across Kyrie's face made everything right with the world. They were fine. It was the world that was fucked up.

Cool night air ruffled Kyrie's fur as he ran at top speed. He felt Fen hot on his heels. It was beyond obvious Fen could overtake him any second. Vampires were faster than Weres. A sexy laugh rang through his head, making the chase twice as hot. He was happy. That was what Kyrie would focus on tonight. No matter what, he had this right now. He felt Fen's intent to jump a half second before he leapt. Kyrie moved to the side, causing Fen to miss him. Using the opportunity to his advantage, Kyrie pounced. His front paws landed on Fen's chest, keeping down his prey. It was obvious he had rolled to bounce back up and ended up in the perfect position for Kyrie's attack.

Got you.

The bright smile Fen wore had Kyrie biting back a dreamy sigh. "It seems you did. What do you intend to do now?" Fen wasn't even winded, proving he had only been toying with Kyrie.

Still, Kyrie played along. *What big teeth you have.*

Fen barked out a laugh. "Isn't that supposed to be my line?"

Maybe, but your fangs are showing. Do I make you hungry? Damn, those fangs barely peeking out had Kyrie primed.

"Famished."

Kyrie immediately turned human. "Then you should take what you want."

Fen's gaze flickered to Kyrie's neck. His eyes glowed for a second.

Pre-cum dripped from Kyrie. He already felt those teeth sinking into his skin, taking them to heaven.

Fen's head lifted. He licked the scar Kyrie proudly wore. It was as if he purposely drew out the anticipation—like foreplay.

A pant burst from Kyrie. With his eyes closed, he savored every brush of Fen's tongue. The smell of the moonlight mixed with his mate's scent. He wanted everything about them to be real so god-damn badly.

Fangs pierced his throat.

The loud cry that left him was out of his control. He was helpless in the arms of this man. His body shook with the ecstasy of release. Kyrie's pleasure mixed with Fen's in his head, stealing his soul.

We are real.

The words sweetly brushed his brain, feeling like the most loving caress. Emotion clogged his throat.

While using nothing but their mixture of cum to ease the way, Fen slowly pushed his way inside Kyrie. It was like neither of them had just blown. They took their time, kissing and straining against each other. The seed of a wishful dream took root as a second orgasm built. Maybe they could be forever. If he worked and fought hard enough, maybe he could be the one who shaped his future. Oxygen disappeared from the world as Fen took him to a whole new plane of bliss. Through the waves that were nothing but elation and spice, Kyrie believed Fen could save him.

Chapter Nine

FEN: *I GOT EVERYTHING moved in and un-packed, so you should be set when you get home.*

Kyrie: *Home. Sigh. I have to admit, I've been skimming your thoughts all night. I love how proud you are of mixing my things with yours. That's so sweet and a definite improvement over all the unhappy customers I've had today.*

Fen: *What's up with the anger lately? Humans are notoriously bad about being unkind to servers.*

Kyrie: *Who knows? At least I get to come home to you every night now.*

Fen: *Thank Goddess.*

Kyrie: *Deidra called and invited us to their house for dinner.*

Fen: *I've never thought about it, but I don't know where they live. Is it in Faerie?*

Kyrie: *Yes and no. They have a house in town for appearance's sake, but there's more house than humans can see.*

Fen: *Can we actually go inside Faerie?*

Kyrie: *I can. Therefore, you can. She and her husband are the only people in town who have always known about me. Fairies can see a person's inner glow. Mine is apparently too bright to hide from them.*

Fen: *That's fascinating. I can't wait to check out the place.*

Fen: *Some nights, guard duty feels very empty and long.*

Kyrie: *I can come hang out with you.*

Fen: *I'd love that.*

The way Fen walked on clouds all the time really justified all his years of yearning for a mate. Kyrie was amazing twenty-four-seven.

"It's probably a good thing Leif left, with all the smiling you do these days."

At just the mention of being happy, Fen wanted to smile even brighter. Bringing Leif into the matter shoved him in between his joy and Leif's pain. He didn't like being in the middle. It was honestly kind of a shitty thing for Stone to say.

But Stone had always been a slight ass when it came to relationships. The guy was bitter and lashed out behind the guise of flirting.

"One has nae to do with the other."

Stone was a gorgeous vampire, and he knew it. He practically smoldered for no reason at all. They had known each other for too many centuries for Fen to fall for any of his bullshit.

"Where is your sexy other half?"

Fen was more than happy to talk about Kyrie. "He's working."

Stone snorted. "You make your mate work? You've lived for as long as I have. The world has always been at your mercy. I know damn well you can more than afford to support your man."

The subject was actually a bit of a sore one for him. He had yet to convince Kyrie to quit. Sometimes, he swore Stone was some sort of enhanced super psychic, seeing even the oldest minds. But they had been turned by the same vampire. Their ages were too similar for Stone to have an advantage. "Kyrie likes to work."

Another loud snort cut through the air. "No one enjoys working, especially such a low-paying peasant job."

Fen's hackles rose a little more. He couldn't show it, though. Fen wouldn't expose his own insecurities about Kyrie's choices. He wouldn't give Stone ammunition to use against him. "I enjoy my position."

Stone clasped his hands behind his back and kept in step with Fen as they patrolled. "That's different. We're warriors for our Goddess. It is an honor to serve."

Fen changed tactics. "Why are you so concerned with my mate?"

A chuckle so low, it was nearly carried away by the wind fell from a mouth that tempted even saints. Not Fen, of course. The strawberry-blond, blue-eyed warrior was too familiar to Fen. "Maybe I find your mate fascinating." Before Fen had time to rip Stone's head from his shoulders, Stone moved on. "Or maybe such a rare pairing should look happier." The statement punched Fen in the chest, undermining the peace he had found. Stone kept talking, oblivious to the inner havoc he wreaked. "All eyes are on you two, studying why you two were chosen. With Waylon, he's a pack leader. It's easier to understand receiving such a blessing. So, why Kyrie? What makes him special?"

Fen tried to stay calm. The last thing he needed to do was give Stone any reason to stay this path. He forced out a laugh. "What? Why would you think there's any crazy explanation? Maybe Odin and Celeste have struck some sort of bargain. Perhaps they are running an experiment. Nae one knows why the deities do anything. We are their creations to do with as they please. It's nae as if any of have any control."

Stone stopped walking and faced Fen.

Fen paused too as the air turned heavier.

The carefree seducer became the hardened and callous warrior. His accent made a rare appearance. "Does that nae enrage you? Are you nae furious about being treated as a toy? All of this," he waved his arm wide, "is nae more than a game and we are the pieces. Just because you currently have what you think you want, that doesn't mean it couldn't change tomorrow on someone else's whim." His stare bored into Fen. "What if this dream life you have isn't real? You're only the second pairing of this experiment, or whatever it is. Maybe the wind will change tomorrow. What will happen then?"

Fen didn't even hesitate. "I'll still sit at Celeste's feet, grateful for having got to taste this. Now I know what it is to have this blessing. Any amount of Kyrie is better than never knowing this happiness exists. I had given up on the dream. You have no idea how close I truly was to choosing the fire." That was a hard admission to make. Vampires were nigh impossible to destroy, but they could choose a warrior's death of walking into the fire. No doubt it was a horrible way to go, but the loneliness had nearly beaten him.

Stone's gaze moved over Fen's face for a second before he dipped his chin and walked away.

Fen didn't move. The conversation bothered him in a way he couldn't explain. It was almost as if Stone knew something he didn't and Fen fucking hated that. A hand landed on Fen's shoulder, startling him. He spun.

Gemini waited, looking calm and not the least bit as if he intended to scare Fen. "You good?"

Fen cleared his throat. "Yeah. Sorry. Just lost in thought."

Gemini smiled. He was truly a good man and simply looked like a nice person... leopard. Of course, he was a snow leopard, the more playful and cuddlier of the species. He was the perfect mate for Frost.

"I wanted to check on you. King Jonathan has sent a crew to give you guys the night off. They showed up a good ten minutes ago and you haven't moved since."

Damn. He really had lost himself in thought. Fen needed someone unbiased to talk to. "Why do you think Celeste put me with a wolf? What's different about us?"

A smile exploded across Gemini's face. "Why was I chosen for such a powerful healer? Who knows? But Celeste doesn't make mistakes. Trust me. She scolded me personally for doubting her by questioning my strength for this position."

"Personally? Wow." Fen didn't think he had heard of that before. "You must have really been making an ass of yourself."

A loud bark of laughter burst from Gemini. It sounded very catlike. "I was, but you didn't have to call me on my shit like that."

Fen realized he was smiling. Happiness had been restored. Life truly was all about who people surrounded themselves with. He needed to be more mindful of that and not let someone else's bitterness destroy his blessings.

"On that note." Fen reached out for Kyrie. He was home and in the shower. Fen barely stopped himself from smirking. "Well, since I'm not needed here, see you later." Fen dissipated and reappeared nude in the shower where his heart waited.

Kyrie didn't startle even as Fen molded against his back. "Mhmm. There he is."

Kyrie reached over his head and held Fen in place as he kissed Kyrie's nape.

Fen hummed against his skin. "Mhmm. There's the spot I've been thinking about all day."

He felt Kyrie chuckle as much as he heard it. The sound vibrated against Fen's lips. "Only that spot?"

He swiped his hand down Kyrie's body. "This one too. I missed you like crazy all day."

Kyrie melted into him. "I missed you too. All I thought about was coming home."

"You do nae have to work, if you recall?" Fen didn't want to ruin the moment. He only wanted Kyrie to know Fen would and could take care of him.

Kyrie slowly turned in Fen's arms. He studied Fen's face. "You know I can hear your thoughts. Feel what you feel. I know this is important to you, but why is this what you want? What would I do all day?"

Fen shrugged. "I'd love to know you're relaxing or playing in the woods." Fen held his stare. "Tasting freedom for once."

Even with water falling, Fen saw the tears fill Kyrie's eyes. Or maybe he just felt them. He couldn't tell the difference any longer.

Kyrie visibly swallowed. "Why?"

Fen knew Kyrie could see his every thought. He knew Kyrie knew the answer. Sometimes there were things that needed to be said. "Because you're mine and I love you."

Kyrie sniffled. "Really?"

He looked so young, standing there begging for someone to love him. "You can reach into my mind anytime you want and see for yourself."

"I love you too."

Elation had Fen near to levitating. He dipped his chin to claim Kyrie's lips and a cold wave of water blasted over him. The oxygen left the room and everything was gone.

Cold iron bars bit into Kyrie's unclothed body. The cage was barely big enough for him to be on his knees, much less stand. It was really no more than a wolf-sized iron kennel. The tears hadn't stopped since the moment he landed in Monnie's temple. While he had known this day would come, he had also prayed his ass off it wouldn't. Things had been going so amazing with Fen. His life with Fen had been nothing but peace and love. The entire time, Kyrie lived with his breath held, waiting every day for the other shoe to drop. He hadn't known exactly what signal Monnie had been waiting for, but Fen's declaration of love fit with his cruelty.

The blond-haired, blue-eyed stunning man who ran this place sat nearby, impatiently waiting for Fen to wake up. Kyrie had never understood how so much beauty could be bestowed upon someone so evil. Monnie made it hard to look away. Maybe that was just what it meant to be a god. Kyrie really hoped Monnie killed him soon. He didn't have much sanity left. Even one more night in this cage would break him.

Unexpectedly, Fen leaped to his feet, ready to fight. His fists were raised and his chest heaved as he eyed the room.

Fury and devastation crossed his features the moment he spotted Kyrie.

You can still dissipate from here. Go now. Don't look back. Kyrie blasted the thoughts at Fen, praying he obeyed.

What's the fuck is going on? I won't leave you.

Monnie popped to his feet. His cocky expression screamed he heard every word. "Boys, there's no need to fight." His gaze locked on Fen. The way his features hardened was terrifying. Kyrie might have scrambled backward if he could move at all. Monnie's arm rose in Kyrie's direction. He slowly closed his fingers into a fist. Kyrie's entire body squeezed like being in a trash compactor. He couldn't even scream. Blood simply poured from his mouth and nose.

Monnie never looked away from Fen. "I don't recommend zapping out of here. All it takes is one more little squeeze, and he's gone."

Fen tried rushing toward Kyrie. He froze in his tracks as if hitting an invisible wall.

Monnie clicked his tongue and shook his head. "There'll be none of that. I don't see why the three of us can't work this out."

"Release my mate." Fen growled the words between clenched teeth, looking more furious than Kyrie had ever seen him.

The pressure released from his body. Kyrie wanted it back the moment Monnie opened his mouth.

"Mate? You think this mutt right here is your mate?" A cruel smile twisted Monnie's lips. "Oh, yeah." He waved his hand and Kyrie's mating marks disappeared. "I forgot. There's no need for those any longer. One of my favorite tricks, if I might add."

Fen looked confused and enraged as fuck.

Go, Fen! Right now. Don't look back.

Monnie's vile gaze locked on Kyrie. A demonic-sounding chuckle filled the air. "He can't hear you. You're not real mates. You know this. It was part of our plan."

Tears flowed freely from Kyrie's eyes, mixing with the blood that wouldn't stop flowing. This was worse than death. Kyrie should have accepted that fate long before Fen got hurt. His only excuse was he was a coward.

"What's going on? Seriously, what is happening right now?"

Fen's anger, hurt and confusion were choking him. Even with Monnie stealing his powers, Kyrie felt the way Fen didn't know what to do. He swallowed past the lump in his throat. "Go. Please go." His voice cracked hard, but there was no way Fen didn't hear.

The squeezing pain returned. "You'll have only his corpse if you try."

A cry tore from Kyrie. The taste of blood felt permanent, but he refused to look away from Fen. "Remember what I said about dreams. You have to go." This was as real as it got. Fen wasn't dreaming, but he needed Fen to believe and leave him behind. A final lie to save Fen from a million others, Kyrie had told. "Go." It was barely a whisper, but it worked. Fen vanished.

The angry roar Monnie released made Kyrie smile.

"Bring him back!"

Kyrie coughed. More blood filled his mouth. His broken bones shifted, nearly knocking him unconscious from the pain, but he wouldn't give Monnie the satisfaction of winning. "I can't." Kyrie laughed. It barely came out as a chuckle and gargled with blood. "You took away my mating marks. He is Celeste's now." He wished like hell there was enough room for him to lie down. His head swam and death's rattle vibrated in his throat.

The way Monnie stormed toward the cage said everything. Kyrie knew he was dead, but he would die knowing he was brave in the end. Better than late than never, he supposed. There were worse fates.

Chapter Ten

TEARS BLURRED KYRIE'S VISION. The pain of having his bones crushed combined with having Fen ripped away from him broke him. It was never ending. He prayed for death. Kyrie should have known Monnie would keep him trapped on the edge, refusing to let him die. Each time Kyrie thought he reached the end, Monnie healed him just enough to start all over again. His mind flitted from one painful event to another. Every life-shattering moment he suffered could have been avoided if Kyrie had been braver. All of this was because he was weak. When he had realized he could escape his life in dreams, the relief had been massive. No way could he have seen this end. Loneliness was a hell of a thing. It drove desperate people to do desperate things. When he had met Monnie, it had been so fucking nice to have his attention. They had spent ages talking. How could he have known Monnie had only sought to know more about Yuri? Yuri was a wolf from town mated to a hellhound. Not just any hellhound, but *the* hellhound—Lucifer's pet. There was nothing Monnie wanted more in the world than to destroy Lucifer. He would go through whoever it took to get to him, but Celeste was a problem. Monnie needed someone free to move between worlds unnoticed. Kyrie would say he was damn unlucky to have Monnie choose him. Unfortunately, it was no accident. He had been groomed for this day.

At first, things hadn't seemed that bad. All he had to do was flirt with Yuri—lure him into the woods and get him alone. Kyrie hadn't known Yuri was already mated. In fact, he hadn't even known the story of Lucifer. Kyrie had only been doing a favor for his new friend. He hadn't realized he was a pawn until he failed. Monnie's fury had been epic. At first, Kyrie had refused to return to Monnie's domain for a while. He had nearly killed himself by staying awake for days. Then the episodes began.

The moment Monnie realized he could take Kyrie's soul without alerting any gods, his life had been over. Monnie had tried the same trick with Fen countless times, only to have Celeste snatch Fen away within minutes. More than that, the longer he tried, the shorter he had him. That game lured Monnie into a new obsession: Fen. Just as it had been with Lucifer, his crazed fixation had never been about love. It was about alleviating the boredom of an endless existence—one he spent in the dreaming, banned—every bit as much as Lucifer had been—from the heavens he used to call home

Not only did Celeste keep him on his toes, constantly forcing him to become more and more creative to see his obsession, somehow Fen resisted him too. No one turned down Monnie's blood and bed while also shaking off his mind control. It was terrifying the lengths Monnie would go to when he wanted something. Nothing was too convoluted or too far. All it had taken was a chance meeting between Kyrie and Fen for Monnie to see a new path: Kyrie.

Kyrie swallowed past the sharp shards of cartilage in his throat. The tears kept flowing. Monnie had sworn once Fen's soul belonged to Kyrie, he would set Kyrie free. After all, he had gotten bored with Kyrie a long time ago. Monnie would create the illusion of mating marks and manipulate Fen's emotions. All Kyrie had to do was make Fen actually love him, stealing him from Celeste's sight. Kyrie would snort if he had the ability any longer. The bargain had seemed like a zero-risk venture on his part. No one ever loved him. The theory of his soul passing to Kyrie with his love and devotion seemed weak to him. With months passing, and no Monnie in sight, Kyrie had started to believe Monnie had lost interest, and maybe, just maybe, Fen somehow was his real mate. Monnie had stopped stealing away with Kyrie's soul, and he had stopped taunting Fen with whispered demands to drive him mad. No way could he have known that Fen saying those three little words would be like throwing the final ingredient into a cauldron, sealing their fate.

His chest stuttered with each painful breath. *Fen.* The tears wouldn't stop. If Kyrie had been smarter, he would have realized how easily he would fall the moment anyone gave him the smallest attention. He hadn't known how amazing Fen would be. Kyrie hadn't known how badly this would hurt. He took another shallow and shaky breath. Kyrie would endure this punishment he had more than earned. Not for Monnie's enjoyment, but as penance for his betrayal. Then maybe he could pass in peace.

The sound of Monnie's pacing beat at his brain. The air crackled with power and rage. Kyrie couldn't even flinch any longer. His torture had turned boring. Now Monnie simply waited. Unfortunately, Kyrie knew for what: for him to heal enough to start all over again. Kyrie kind of wanted to laugh. Physical pain meant nothing anymore. His spirit was broken. He had nothing left to give.

A bright light burst through the room between Monnie and him, temporarily blinding him. The deadly growl that assaulted his ears had Kyrie trying harder to see.

"You dare touch my son! Mine?"

"Freyr. I—"

Monnie's body lifted from the ground—like he was no more than a child. Kyrie's vision faded, but not before he heard Monnie's pained screams along with the wet and popping noises of limbs being ripped away. Everything went black.

With his heart in his throat, Frost locked himself in his office and tried to calm his nerves. For too long, he had thought of Kyrie's advice to confront Celeste. Every time he had gotten close to a decision on whether that was something he wanted to do, he always took the coward's path. Maybe some things were better off staying unsaid.

Tears of frustration beat at the backs of his eyes. He didn't know himself any longer. His life had become so out-of-control since he moved to Wulfe, Frost wondered if he would wake up one day and learn this was all some type of crazy dream. That thought alone was enough to send him over the edge. He couldn't live like this. Frost couldn't wake up and learn Gemini was just a fantasy. Gemini was everything. The only thing. Without him, Frost didn't want to exist. He couldn't.

Frost closed his eyes and took a breath. *Jonathan.*

Yo.

Despite everything, Frost smiled at the nearly eight-foot golden Nephilim's nonchalant response to Frost's mental call. *Would it be okay if we talked?*

We're talking now, so yeah.

Frost shook his head and chuckled. He thought he had issues, but he couldn't even imagine Jonathan's experience. One day, he had been a normal, everyday journalist, and the next, boom. He was the Nephilim king of the Americas, ruling the land of supernatural creatures.

I meant in person. Something isn't quite right. His claim brought an eerie silence.

Right when he worried he had been abandoned, Jonathan was back. *Lire is on his way to guide you.*

Relief poured through Frost. One hurdle crossed. Maybe he would lose his nerve the moment he set eyes on Jonathan. It was possible Jonathan had no more answers than Frost. He had to do something. There was no way he could go to Celeste. Not to mention, he didn't want to sound accusing. There was a very real chance Kyrie was wrong about him. What could a barely-an-adult wolf know that no one else did?

Frost's door exploded open, sending Frost scrambling from his chair and fully prepared for an attack. A very nude, chest-heaving Fen stood in the destroyed doorway, holding an equally nude Kyrie.

"Fix him."

Frost forgot his own worries as the healer inside him took control. This was his purpose. That much Frost knew was real.

Nothing felt real. Fen didn't pace. He wasn't sure he even breathed. Fen damn sure never thought he would see the day he would sit inside King Jonathan's home, watching his mate slip away. He couldn't reach Kyrie. It was like they had never met, and Fen stared at a dying stranger. Yet his heart hurt, and he thought his chest might cave. He loved Kyrie. That much was real, even if everything else made no sense right now. He needed Kyrie's eyes to open. Nothing would be right again until he knew Kyrie's soul was back where it belonged: with Fen.

Fen went over every moment of the past few months in his head, all the way to the moment he woke up on the floor of his shower alongside a not breathing Kyrie. He had never been more confused or scared. Kyrie had caught him in such a whirlwind, Fen had forgotten all about Kyrie's mystery illness and the time Kyrie called Jörmungandr Monnie—like they were friends. What he had witnessed wasn't friendship, and Fen hated himself for all the things he had simply forgotten. His angel had needed him, and Fen had been so caught up in his own happiness, he had failed his mate. Kyrie hadn't had another incident of not waking up since their mating. He had pushed the incidents from his mind. Fen had told himself it was just dehydration or something and went on with life. Now he listened to Kyrie's heartbeat get slower by the hour, and the most powerful people he knew couldn't do anything but try to seek answers from Celeste. In the meantime, all Fen could do was wait and pray Frost could find out what no one else could. It felt like a million years passed. He needed Kyrie to open his eyes and explain everything. Everything inside Fen begged for whatever plan Monnie claimed they had hatched to be all bullshit and had nothing to do with their relationship. This had to be a sick, cruel joke. He wouldn't feel this strongly unless they were real. This waiting to know the truth and to hear the entire story choked the life from him. Fen worried he might be the one whose heart stopped. He had never been so exhausted, and he couldn't figure out why. As a vampire, even this massive amount of stress, fear, and sadness shouldn't make him this worn down. Fen hadn't felt this way since he was a new turn.

The sound of Kyrie's soft heartbeat hypnotized him. Fen's eyes slid closed. He just needed to rest for half a second, then he could get back to hovering and maybe start some pacing. His head bobbed. He sucked in a sharp gasp, startled by his dozing. His eyes shot open. He blinked. Kyrie was gone. Not passed. Just not there. He blinked again. The bed was still empty. Alarms blared as the king's perimeter was breached. Fen jumped to his feet. His panicked gaze shot in every direction. The blaring stopped, but Fen's terror didn't.

Frost rushed into the room. He immediately focused on the bed. His shoulders sagged. "I was afraid of that."

"Of what? What happened? Where is my mate?" The shouted words were beyond his control. He couldn't lower his voice. The fear was real. Every loss was too big. He was tired of staying calm when it was obviously time to panic.

Frost moved to the bed and sat. "I have no idea." He looked defeated, which didn't give Fen hope. "My guess is his body rejoined his soul."

Fen's brain hurt. The frustration had him ready to tear down the world. His blood boiled. Someone had to start answering questions soon or he couldn't be held responsible for his actions. "What the fuck does that even mean?"

Frost rubbed his temples, as if his head pounded, and he dealt with his own existential crisis. "Jörmungandr had Kyrie's soul."

"I know that goddamn much."

Fen's rage didn't seem to penetrate whatever inner crisis Frost endured. Frost simply kept talking as if Fen hadn't said a word. "As soon as Celeste heard, she sent word to Freyr. It seems he maybe ripped off Jörmungandr's legs or something like that. Unfortunately, they'll grow back, but Freyr ensured Kyrie's safety. As soon as the news dropped, I raced in here, in case he needed me when his soul returned to his body. It seems it went the opposite way."

Fen sat. "I don't understand any of that. Went the opposite way? Does that mean he's still in the dreaming? I don't know what's happening right now."

"Yeah, me either, really." Frost stared into space, sounding as defeated as Fen felt. "There for a while, I really thought I was making a difference—that I was helping. Every day, I feel a little more useless." Frost flashed him a wry smile. "I'm sure you don't care about any of that, and it probably doesn't make you feel any better." The smile disappeared. "I'm sorry I failed you. Apparently, that's what I do now."

"It's okay to be sad, but it's not okay to give up."

Fen and Frost's head whipped toward the open doorway. A beautiful, angelic-looking blond stood, waiting for their attention while twisting a ragged-looking doll and looking unsure of his welcome.

"Hey, Tam." Frost still sounded beyond saving, but he obviously knew their visitor.

Tam took a small step into the room. His eyes darted between them. He reminded Fen of a skittish animal, looking for any excuse to run away. Suddenly, Tam's heaven-colored eyes focused on Fen. All hints of innocence and uncertainty disappeared. Pure, unadulterated power stared at him. "Maybe I am an animal."

Fuck. It seemed Tam was powerful. Even a mind as old as Fen's didn't stand a chance of hiding any thoughts from him. "I didn't mean to offend you."

A bright smile lit Tam's face. "You didn't." In a flash, too quick for the eye to see, Tam was a tiny white fox. He bounced from wall to wall and furniture to furniture like a fox on crack. He was back to human every bit as quickly. The odd part was, Fen knew damn well this was no Werefox. Weres couldn't shift while wearing clothes and still have clothes at the end. He was so much stronger than any creature Fen had ever met ... and dangerous. Tam practically crackled with untapped power.

He sat on the floor and hugged his doll the way a child would do. Fen recognized the act for what it was. Tam knew he was the most powerful being in the room, but he seemed to want them to understand they weren't in danger. Tam's focus locked on Frost. "You didn't fail. You're just sad and worried about Gemini. It's bleeding into everything else. Trust me, I do that all the time too. The mind doesn't care about the truth or how badly you want to be normal like everyone else. But you're not failing Gemini or at being a healer. He didn't lose anything by being paired with you. He gained everything. When I met Risk, I refused to accept that he could love me, since I was just this broken thing that crawled from Hell. I didn't want to taint him." Tam stared at nothing for a moment. "Still don't, actually." He shook his head, as if shaking off a trance. "But those thoughts aren't real. They're make believe."

Fen tried his ass off to keep his mind blank, but there was a lot of information in that lecture that only led to more questions. Apparently, Tam had crawled from Hell and had a mate named Risk. Fen gathered that much.

Tam kept talking, ignoring any thoughts Fen might have let slip through. "You need to face the truth. You keep thinking you're this human who got tossed into a position you can't achieve. The reality is—you've never been human. You've always been part of our world. Someone hid you behind a human glamour. Maybe it was the right thing to do at the time. There's no way I can know. But there was never any chance you could escape your true identity. There was no way to ignore the fact that you can't die and magic and power runs through your blood. You would have eventually found us, no matter what else happened in your life. There's no escaping fate." Tam went from serious to chipper so fast, it nearly made Fen's head spin. "Plus, you're my cousin or something like that and I would've come for you and dragged you to Wulfe so you could find your mate. I really need to sit down and think about this family tree business." He seemed to turn inward. Tam used his fingers as if counting. "I'm Michael's son and Michael is Celeste's grandson. So, I'm Celeste's great-grandson. Lucifer is Celeste's twin and you're his son. So, you're my cousin, right?"

He looked Fen's way with his brow furrowed. "It is cousin, right?"

Thankfully, the total shock hadn't rendered Fen totally mute. "Yeah. That sounds right."

Tam brightened as he focused on Frost again. "See. You can't escape us."

Frost looked as if his soul took a hike. There was no one home. He stared at nothing and had zero reaction. It was like his body was in suspended animation.

Tam stood, seemingly oblivious to the bomb he dropped. "Anyhow. Stop thinking all of this is some big mistake or dream. Gemini loves you. He doesn't think he got screwed out of some normal life with kids and a less dangerous spouse. You're exactly what he wants and you're exactly where you're supposed to be. In fact, you're a pretty kick-ass healer. Don't blame yourself for not knowing Monnie held Kyrie's soul hostage. No one could've known that. Even Granny Celeste was in the dark. I mean, Monnie is a pretty crafty god in his own right. Plus, the gods don't spend their days in each other's business or anything like that. Just ask your dad. They just do their thing."

Frost cleared his throat. His voice came out sounding gruff. "Yeah. I'll ask."

With a smile and a wave, Tam trounced away, singing something at the top of his lungs about bashing mice on the head.

Fen looked Frost's way.

Frost stared at nothing again.

"Are you okay?"

Frost cleared his throat. "Yeah. Just making a mental list of all the people who've lied to me and used me."

Before Fen could respond, a visibly enraged Gemini strode through the door, looking more badass than Fen had ever seen him. Gemini had always struck him as more of a lover than a fighter. Fen saw the strength Celeste obviously counted on now. His eyes were terrifying. He didn't acknowledge Fen. His angry steps carried him to Frost. "I've had enough." He snatched Frost from the bed and tossed him over his shoulder, leaving Fen behind.

That was fine. Fen had some rage to deal with too—like how dare Monnie fuck with his mate? That soul belonged to Fen. Mating mark or not, Kyrie was his other half. Fuck the gods and their bullshit. Just as Gemini appeared to be done with their shit, Fen was too. Kyrie was his. How fucking dare anyone claim otherwise? Fen stood. It was time to find his man.

Chapter Eleven

THE PUDDLE BENEATH HIM rippled as Kyrie patted it with his paw. He didn't want to think. He wanted to wolf. Just wolf. His sanity demanded he cling to his animal side and do the simple animal things. No drama or heartache. Just play in nature and pretend his shattered heart wouldn't kill him. He could chase bugs and eat rabbits. A shudder ran through Kyrie. Maybe he could lead the way into wolf vegetarianism. He felt sick at just the idea of a tiny life burning out in his mouth. In the human world, he could pretend all his meat came from the Acme factory as it was cooked to a safe temperature. Kyrie had never been a very good wild animal. He had never been very good at anything.

The grass rustled next to him. Kyrie didn't even bother to look. Nothing could happen to him that hadn't been done before. He was too tired to care. The hairy legs of a bear appeared beside him before turning into the hairy legs of a man. Strong fingers ran through his fur. Kyrie closed his eyes and fought not to cry. He was wrong. One thing hadn't been done to him. He hadn't been comforted. Kyrie wasn't sure he didn't prefer the torture.

"My pack rejected me when I fell in love with Leif."

Kyrie didn't open his eyes, but he shuffled a little closer.

Aspen kept petting him. His voice sounded like his mind was far away. "I don't think he ever truly grasped how much I sacrificed for him. Vampires don't feel the same sense of community as Weres. Maybe they form their own pack or team, but it's not the same. They don't lean on each other the way animal packs do. Not that any of this matters now. Nothing has for a long time. I don't really know what I'm getting at. Do you want to run away with me? I don't really have anyone or anything holding me anywhere anymore."

The first tear fell. Kyrie honestly couldn't recall the last time he cried without shame tainting every tear, and—oddly—the tears weren't for him. They were for the shattered heart and spirit behind each word Aspen spoke.

Kyrie tilted his head so he could see Aspen's face. *He's a fool.*

A small smile played on Aspen's lips. "Why am I not the least bit surprised you can do that? You practically glow with power."

Kyrie no longer cared what happened to him. It didn't matter if the whole world knew him. *I'm not special. It's a curse to hear everyone.*

Aspen nodded. "I imagine it is. As much as I've prayed and begged the gods for Leif to be my true mate, I'm a little grateful I can't hear him. It's bad enough to know he hates me. If I had to hear how deeply that loathing runs, who knows what I might do?"

You'd lie here and smack puddles the way I am because the knowing fucking breaks you.

Aspen took an audibly deep breath.

Kyrie didn't force Aspen to come up with some bullshit placations. *Where should we go?*

Aspen chuckled. "As far as we can drive on two hundred bucks and an old, beat-up pickup truck, I suppose."

A hint of life returned. He could help Aspen. Maybe he still had some purpose. *I could take you to Leif and you could bite him.*

"I have no clue where to even look."

Hold on a second. Kyrie shifted and settled deeper into the grass. He whisper-barked into the weeds, calling on the fairies for help. He would owe them a favor, but if Aspen found the happiness Kyrie never would, then it was worth it. Tiny voices only he could hear filled his ears. Kyrie whispered back his thanks.

Leif is camping one town over, fishing and reconnecting with nature.

"Reconnecting with nature?"

Yeah. I don't know. Fairies can be kind of dreamy and poetic.

"You were talking to fairies."

You can too. They're all over this forest. Just because you can't see them doesn't mean they can't see you.

Aspen looked horrified. "That's actually a bit disturbing. I've spent a lot of time as an animal the last few months. They see everything?"

Yeah. They don't give a shit what you're doing. They're too busy fucking. The more Kyrie spoke, the better he felt. A simple conversation about nothing felt normal in a way nothing had in a long time. He turned human and sat back on his heels. "Seriously. I can take you to Leif. It might not make any difference, but I'm actually more powerful than him. I'm not hiding my powers anymore, since I don't really care if they catch anyone's attention who might kill me. I could hold him in place while you whale on him."

Aspen laughed. His smile brightened Kyrie's mood. "I'm not sure that would make any difference." He paused. His smile turned genuine as he held Kyrie's stare. "I'd honestly love to get out of this town, though. The knowing and judgmental eyes are crushing me."

Kyrie nodded. "It hurts too much here."

They never looked away from each other.

"Vegas," they said simultaneously before falling into laughter.

Kyrie stood. Clothes appeared, covering his skin. "Vegas." He held his hand out for Aspen. The world really was Kyrie's oyster now. At least until using his full powers got him stricken down by some vengeful demon or whatever.

He doubted Monnie would risk crossing Kyrie's dad again. Kyrie had not seen that one coming. But considering Freyr had zapped him back home without a word, he supposed nothing had changed as far as family went. He had gone numb to that bullshit a long time ago. Now he had to find a way to live with the loss of Fen while knowing it was one hundred percent his fault. He couldn't think about all the ways he had betrayed the man he loved. Those thoughts would shatter him past the point of repair. He was a master at disassociating. Kyrie could focus everything he possessed on Aspen's problems. He could probably eke out a couple of hours before the pain caught him and crippled him again. He would spend those hours trying to bring joy to Aspen. Maybe he would whip up a big win for Aspen in one of the casinos. His final act of kindness before he chose to move on to the next realm. Maybe that gesture would be enough to bring him peace. Otherwise, nothing would.

Returning to Wulfe turned out to be a lot harder than Fen expected. Since no one except a very select high-on-the-list members of Jonathan's team could dissipate in or out of Jonathan's land, his choices had been to cut through the mirrors or walk to the road to zap out. Either way took him through the absolute uproar happening throughout Jonathan's house. It seemed no one, but likely Celeste, had known about Frost. They had all been fed the same information and had no reason to question his parentage. Each yelled sentence, someone looked Tam's way and ensured he knew they weren't mad at him. Tam had simply held his doll and nodded. Jonathan wasn't there for whatever reason, but Fen wouldn't be surprised to learn he had known if Tam had. Honestly, the Lucifer news explained a lot. Druids were considered highly powerful and dangerous due to their secrecy and their ability to stay hidden from everyone and everything, including the deities. They could cloak miles of land and live an invisible and peaceful existence. But no one had known any of that about Frost, and Frost probably also didn't know he could do those things. So they had all run with the idea that he was a rare find. Not only was he important, but he was at high risk of anything with evil intentions, absconding with him and wreaking havoc on the world. Frost being half human made him especially vulnerable. Now it looked like he had never been half human either. He was born of a druid and the king of Hell. The king of Hell bit was a lot to swallow in one sitting.

Now, it seemed, Gemini had taken Frost home and then vanished. Fen's head hurt now, and he was aggravated with the lies and secrets. Thankfully, that irritation had pushed him to march straight to the road after learning all the crazy deceptions. He thought maybe Leif, Frost, and Gemini had the right idea. Maybe it was time he took his maybe-mate and ran. They had earned it.

Fen sat the moment he walked through the door. From his couch, he eyed the life he shared with Kyrie. There were clothes still on the floor from Fen attacking Kyrie when he couldn't take the heat between them anymore. Granted, they had been putting together a puzzle at the time. He had never withstood the torture of watching Kyrie bite his bottom lip while focused on the pieces. Goddess, he loved everything about Kyrie. Fen couldn't lose him. He had to find him. His nerves were so bad, his neck itched. He practically felt the way Kyrie blamed himself. The absolute knowledge Kyrie was out there somewhere, hating himself for betraying Fen—like he had a choice—had Fen back on his feet. If Kyrie didn't know Fen loved him too much to let them go, then that was a failing on Fen's part. He had to show Kyrie how real love didn't quit, even if it was found and not given.

Without a single thought, Fen dissipated and reappeared in Vegas. He recognized the fake sky that was actually pretty nice to look at. He had been hypnotized by it the first time he came here. Kyrie's blood still pumped through Fen's veins. Fen followed that trail. His pace increased as he felt the distance between them close. Kyrie came into view at a slot machine with a drink in one hand. His whole demeanor screamed he was drunk. That was a hell of a feat, considering he likely burned through alcohol like it was nothing. Of course, his dad was the good-time god, so maybe he had passed on some traits that let him feel the effects of drinking.

Kyrie's gaze shot in his direction. Even through his obvious shock, his eyes still burned with longing. How could he think there was any chance Fen could walk away from this? No one had ever looked at him the way Kyrie did. He had no clue how many lies he had been fed, but there were some things a person couldn't fake. Actual love was one of those things, and Kyrie loved him. He didn't know what Kyrie saw in Fen's expression as Fen's long stride ate up the space between. No doubt he looked as crazed as he felt. Either Kyrie had accepted his fate or he knew Fen would never hurt him because he didn't run. He damn well better know he was safe with Fen.

No words were spoken. Fen snagged the back of Kyrie's neck and hauled him forward. He took the kiss he wanted, pouring all his fear into it. Kyrie didn't hesitate to kiss Fen back every bit as aggressively.

When he was certain he had made his point, Fen pulled away, but he didn't release Kyrie. "How dare you run away and leave me scared as fuck? I had to stand by and watch you tortured. Then I thought I was about to watch you die and then you just vanished. Next, I find you in a fucking casino, drinking and gambling like nothing happened. What the fuck, Kyrie? I can't decide if I did something to make you think I'd quit us that easily, or if you already have?"

Tears filled Kyrie's eyes.

Fen wasn't done. "I did exactly what you wanted. When you told me to trust you and leave, I left and got help. What about that screamed I was done? Just what the fuck? Did you honestly think I would just leave you? If so, I don't know what I've done wrong, but it was obviously something."

Tears spilled over Kyrie's lashes and rolled down his cheeks. "You still have our mating mark."

Fen's eyes flickered to Kyrie's neck. "Yeah. You do too. I knew you would. That fucked-up God can erase all he wants in a dream, but he can't change our reality. He can't take away our blessing from Celeste. Here, in real life, you're mine. If you ever run away from me again, I'm turning you over my knee. Do you understand? For fuck's sake, you're gambling." He couldn't let that part go.

Kyrie took a shaky-sounding breath. "I thought you wouldn't want me anymore. I thought you would hate me."

"Over my fucking knee," Fen reminded him through clenched teeth.

Kyrie sniffled. "I feel like this is where I should say 'yes, Daddy'."

Happiness and relief exploded through Fen. There was the man Fen had fallen in love with. The one who used humor when life got to be too much.

"Oh, hey. You showed up. I knew you would eventually."

Fen's chin shot up.

Aspen pulled out a stool at the slot machine next to Kyrie. He put his rewards card into the machine and a voucher. He looked relaxed. Aspen hit the highest bet button. The machine made a loud sound—like a motor starting followed by dings before going back to motors. Aspen didn't look at whatever it was doing. His gaze stayed locked on Fen.

"You look like hell."

Fen glanced down at himself. He had borrowed clothes from one of Jonathan's guards. He hadn't brushed his hair since Kyrie and his interrupted shower. It was very possible he looked as if he had rolled around on the floor. His last twenty-four hours had been an absolute nightmare.

A loud alarm made Aspen jump. His gaze slid toward the machine. He looked totally shook. "Um. I'm pretty sure I just won four-point-three million dollars. That can't be right."

Kyrie turned and leaned over to look at the screen. "Seriously? I didn't even know that game paid out that high." A loud bark of laughter escaped Kyrie as he eyed the machine. "Holy shit. You won four-point-three million dollars!"

Fen stared at Kyrie's profile. He was a hell of an actor. His surprise looked genuine. *You're amazing.*

Kyrie's gaze slid Fen's way. A small smile touched his lips. *He's a big bear. It'll take a lot of money if he hopes to chase Leif.*

Warmth spread through Fen's chest. Kyrie believed in love winning, whether he realized it or not. *What if they genuinely aren't true mates?*

What if we weren't? Kyrie shot back.

Touché. I'd absolutely still chase you to the ends of the earth and back until you gave in and kept me.

Kyrie's eyes glimmered. *Don't worry. I wouldn't make you chase me. I love you too much.*

Fen nodded as if they spoke aloud. *You still owe me all the explanations, though.* He immediately wished he hadn't said anything. At least, not yet.

Sadness filled Kyrie's expression. "Aye."

Fen's bright smile was back. "Are you mocking my accent again?"

"Maybe."

Damn. I get the feeling you really do want me to turn you over my knee.

Sexual promise lit Kyrie's features. *If you promise you're really mine forever, I'll let you do whatever you want, Daddy.*

The desire that slammed into him nearly knocked Fen off his feet. "This is forever. Do nae fucking forget it again." Even Fen heard the lust with a biting edge in his voice. He hauled Kyrie, stool and all, against him. When he wrapped his arms around his mate, the truth set into stone inside him. He genuinely didn't blame Kyrie even an ounce for Monnie's insane bullshit. Kyrie was a victim to the whims of a merciless god every bit as much as Fen had been. Even a god hadn't stood a chance against them, though. Not as long as they had each other. But Kyrie needed to let Fen check him for injuries soon, or Fen couldn't promise Kyrie wouldn't get that spanking. The day had swung too wildly. His insides still shook hard enough to make him sick. A lot of his calm was an act. They needed time alone with no human witnesses. His soul craved its other half, and Fen didn't think he could hold it back.

With a half-smoked cigar hanging from his mouth, Leif watched the excitement surrounding Aspen. Shock practically bled from Aspen's pores. Leif chuckled. There was a hard mass in the center of Leif's chest where his heart should be. Despite that, he still couldn't look away. Of course, he had come here for exactly this: a single glance of the bear he couldn't shake.

"Can I get you anything?"

Leif checked over his shoulder and in the direction of the voice. A blonde human server waited for a response. "No, thanks. I'm good."

"I'll bet."

Leif smiled, hoping not to be rude. He appreciated her hungry tone, but Leif also knew it wasn't personal. Vampires gave off pheromones that lured humans to them, making it easier for them to feed.

She moved closer and sat on the stool next to him. "Which one has you looking so intense? You haven't looked away from those three the entire time you've been here." She nodded toward Aspen, Kyrie, and Fen across the room. "You know we're not supposed to bring free drinks to people who aren't actively gambling."

Without breaking eye contact, Leif pressed a button on his machine, casting his bet. "You don't have to worry." He tossed a quick glance Aspen's way, making sure he didn't lose sight of him before focusing on the server again. "The one who just hit the jackpot is my ex."

She made a show of sneaking a peek Aspen's way as well. "Nice choice. Are you stalking him?"

Leif didn't miss a beat. "Yes."

She laughed. Her blue eyes swam with mirth. Admittedly, she was extremely beautiful, but Aspen owned his heart. "I could take him a drink, if you'd like. I don't have to say who it's from."

The idea of Aspen not knowing it was him was irresistible. "You don't happen to have Jack Daniel's Tennessee Honey, do you?"

The blonde's smile grew. "We do."

"That's his favorite." There was no missing the tinge of sadness in his voice.

The server stood and squeezed his shoulder. "I'm on it."

Leif stared so hard at Aspen, waiting for the drink to arrive, that his eyes burned from the need to blink. Finally, he saw the blonde server approach. He watched her mouth move while she held out the glass. The loud-ass machines around him made it impossible—even with preternatural hearing—to make out what was said.

Aspen's fingers wrapped around the glass. He froze as her words hit.

The server walked away while Aspen still held the drink as if locked in the position of accepting it. It was like Aspen's body refused to move.

Leif couldn't watch anymore. He glanced at his screen and hit the button again. Lights flashed and made noises like he was about to win and then he didn't. His throat swelled. He shouldn't have sent that drink. All he had accomplished was rekindling the false hope he had carried for years. Weres and vampires were suddenly being paired as true mates. Hopeless love sat so heavily on his chest, he couldn't breathe. Surely it would have already happened to them if it was meant to be. Despite his best efforts, Leif's gaze slid back Aspen's way. The untouched drink sat on the now empty machine. All three men were gone. He wasn't surprised. That big of a win likely meant he had to fill out paperwork or something. The pressure at the backs of his eyes increased. The lump in his throat grew bigger. It seemed Aspen had finally given up on him. Leif had finally broken him with his refusal to bend.

A solid but cozy warmth pressed against his back. Leif's heart stopped. He would know that chest in a dark room filled with strangers at an orgy. Then the sweet yet wild scent of the man he loved overcame him. The crushed pieces of his soul jangled, reminding him of what it felt like to lose Aspen all over again.

Aspen nuzzled his neck, audibly drawing in Leif's scent. When warm lips softly brushed his skin, Leif's eyes automatically closed to savor the sensation. He didn't want any other senses interfering with the feel of perfect lips on his skin. His chest felt like it was being stomped on by buffalo.

"I can't beg anymore. Either come back to me where you belong or stay gone. I can't go another night thinking you might sleep in my arms again. Don't tease me with some half-life where you give me just enough hope to keep me hanging on. My sanity can't handle this anymore." Another sweet kiss brushed his neck while Leif sat frozen by the love that choked him. The tender arms that had taken him to heaven thousands of times gently squeezed him one final time. "Whatever you decide, you'll always be my prickly pear."

The blow was massive. Cuddly bear and prickly pear. The ridiculous pet names still haunted his dreams. Aspen's softly spoken words, meant for his ears alone, were the last he would get of Aspen. Aspen's warmth disappeared as quickly and quietly as it appeared. Leif was left with nothing but chill bumps and agony. A little rage, too. Aspen was the one who threw them away. He was the one who said he couldn't live with waking up another day knowing that day might be the one they lost each other. Leif would have stayed forever if Aspen hadn't tossed him out of his life. Now

Aspen was back. Leif didn't know if he could survive it.

"Would you like something to drink, sweetie?"

Leif glanced over his shoulder, fighting the pains in his chest. It was a different server. Maybe he needed the comfort. "Yeah. Can I get a Jack Daniel's Tennessee Honey?" He wanted to grab one last hint of Aspen.

"Sorry, honey. We don't have that. I can get you an Old Forester."

Leif stared at the woman for a moment before his gaze slid toward where Aspen had left his glass. It was gone. He blinked, wondering if he hallucinated the last half hour of his life. Maybe he just needed to feed. It was possible he was simply losing his mind.

Chapter Twelve

THEY COULD HAVE GONE home. A still shocked Aspen had been given a penthouse suite for the night. Surprisingly, Fen had been the one to agree when Aspen invited them to stay. No matter how hard Kyrie tried, his muscles wouldn't unclench. Maybe he braced for the worst since dealing with Monnie's torture, but Kyrie knew better. Fen hadn't torn into him yet—like he deserved—and Kyrie waited for Fen's rage to strike him. The truth could still very well destroy them.

Instead, Fen lovingly undressed Kyrie and checked for any lingering injuries or bruises. "Do you want to tell me the story?"

"Do I? No. But you're owed, so..."

Fen's sexy green eyes collided with his. "You don't owe me anything. I saw him hurting you. You endured that for me. You took the punishment so I could escape. I have a feeling you did it, even though you didn't believe I would get help."

Kyrie's guilty gaze hit his lap.

"I'm nae coward."

Kyrie's chin shot up. "No. I would never think that. You're amazing." Fen had to believe him, or Kyrie couldn't live with himself. "I just thought you finally agreed to go because Monnie made you hate me."

"No." Fen stroked Kyrie's face with the back of his knuckles. "Confused me, aye. But no one has the power to make me stop loving you. With that said, I would like to know what the fuck just happened."

As Kyrie had said, Fen deserved to know. "After Neo died, my best friend," Kyrie reminded him in case he didn't remember. "I was too scared to make friends again. Plus, I immediately became a pariah. Everyone knew I had gotten Neo and his family killed. They just didn't know how or why. People literally crossed the street when they saw me. All I did was work and sleep, trying to get through every day until I could save enough to get out of that town."

Fen crawled onto the bed and tugged Kyrie into his arms. "I assume you were afraid to use your powers."

Kyrie nodded against Fen's chest. "Using my powers is the reason Neo is dead. I'd just kind of discovered I could do some strange things—like I was growing into my powers. No one had warned me not to use them. Hell, I didn't even know what I was using. Then I was alone in the world... kind of."

"Monnie?"

Kyrie nodded again. He knew Fen could reach into his mind and scoop out his life's details. Kyrie appreciated Fen allowing him to skip the ugly bits. "One night, during the full moon run, everyone else was laughing and whatnot in the woods. I could hear them in the distance, and I was lonelier than ever. I thought hard about using my curse again."

"Curse?"

"That's how I've always seen this half of me that destroys everything." Kyrie swallowed. He didn't want to cry anymore. "Anyhow, I was kind of pouncing, playing with frogs at the edge of the stream, and a snake appeared. The way the air popped, I knew he was more than the serpent he pretended. No sooner than I had that thought, he turned into this beautiful man." Kyrie winced at his own words. "Sorry."

Fen kissed the top of his head. "Don't be. I've seen him. He's literally a god. I'd say that's as close to the epitome of perfection as a being can be. It's no reflection of his soul."

Kyrie took a deep breath, trying to let go of some of the stress still stiffening his bones. "For the first time in a long time, I had a friend. He's the one who told me who I am and to stay hidden. I believed him because why wouldn't I? The only people I ever considered family were dead because of me. So that was definitely validation for me that I had been right to live as a lone wolf." Kyrie had only meant to touch the bare bones of his history with Monnie.

Unfortunately, he couldn't stop trying to justify every decision he had made.

"Plus, Monnie is a god. Of course, he knew better than me. He told me about my father and gave me roots I never felt as if I had. As I said, he was my friend... until he wasn't anymore. His requests for favors became demands and then moved to abuse when I didn't comply."

Fen tensed as if he fought the urge to fight on Kyrie's behalf.

Kyrie stroked his stomach and kept talking. If he didn't get this out now, he never would. "He wanted information on Lucifer, but I had no way of getting that. Then Yuri became Riku's guardian wolf and Monnie hatched a plan."

"He wanted you to seduce Yuri straight into his clutches under the nose of Celeste."

"Exactly. Of course, there was no chance of that and the punishments broke me. One way or another, I was done. When I tried to break away from our friendship, he simply stole me in my sleep, pulling me into the dreaming anytime he pleased. I didn't know my body was being left behind lifeless until you took me to Frost." Kyrie paused and cleared his throat. They were coming to the part he hated the most. "When the whole showdown between Lucifer, Celeste, and Monnie went down, things quieted for a minute. I thought I was free. Of course, as it turned out, chasing you had lit a fire in him, and he found a new fixation."

Kyrie tilted his chin up and met Fen's stare. "I swear I never wanted you to get hurt. After you took me to Frost that first time, I tried to pick a fight and run away. I decided to let Monnie kill me. But then you said I was the reason food tasted good again and fuck. My needy heart took control. In a flash, I had never wanted anything more than to be with you. I thought I could just play along and maybe we could figure things out when I got brave enough to tell you everything. Then Monnie disappeared again, and I let my ridiculous, greedy soul pretend he had found a new game elsewhere. There was no way I could've known you saying you loved me was the spring of his trap. Well, you know what happened after that."

"Love."

"What?"

Fen held him tighter. "You said loved—like it's in the past. I swear my love is very much present."

Kyrie drew a shaky breath. "I love you too." He held his breath, wondering if they would magically drop again.

Fen rolled, tucking Kyrie beneath him. His beautiful eyes stared down at Kyrie with nothing but honesty and love shining in them. "It's my turn."

Kyrie had no idea what that meant, but he was onboard.

Even though Fen knew everyone colored stories in a way that made them look the least guilty, he didn't care. The solid facts were Monnie was a full fledge true blue from nearly the beginning of time god. Kyrie had never stood a chance of freeing himself from Monnie's plotting. Truthfully, he should kiss that fucked-up god right on the mouth for orchestrating the greatest pairing in the history of the world. But Kyrie needed to hear Fen's side of the story so he could let go of the ugly bits.

He skimmed his lips across Kyrie's mouth before settling his weight so Kyrie couldn't get away while he talked. "That night you realized Yuri already had a mate—as I've told you—I desperately regret not going on that full moon run with you. I thought about you a lot afterwards, and I tried to organically run into you all the time, but you were never around." Fen cleared his throat. Things were about to take a turn. "When I showed up at your job, I knew you worked there. More than that, I knew you were working that night. I purposely didn't come in until the end of your shift." He didn't give Kyrie a chance to ask. "Yeah. I knew what time your shift ended because I was sort of kind of stalking you." Fen winced.

Kyrie chuckled.

The sound spurred him to keep going. "I was honestly taken aback by your age. Your eyes have always looked like they've seen too much, even when you're smiling." He swiped the hair away from Kyrie's face, savoring Kyrie's beauty. "Something happened to me that night by the fire. Your smile snapped something to life inside me." As much as Fen didn't want to make all the confessions, Kyrie had earned them. "I'd been dangerously close to choosing a warrior's death for a while before you came along. You just smiled. That was all it took. I knew I wanted to wake up to that smile for the rest of my life." He shook his head. "Please don't ever consider taking that away from me again. I need you to learn how to talk to me and not run away. There was no life in me before you. I won't choose to cling to it if you're gone."

Kyrie cupped his face. "You have my word."

Fen felt and heard his honesty. "I believe." He lowered his head and kissed Kyrie.

Kyrie moved just enough to speak. "You should make love to me to seal the deal."

"Have no doubt. That's exactly my plan." As he kissed a path down Kyrie's body, Fen realized—once again—they were in a position where there was no lube.

A bark of laughter burst from Kyrie. He obviously heard Fen's disgruntled thought. Kyrie snapped his fingers. Not only did he hold a bottle of lube, but their clothes disappeared.

Fen accepted the bottle. "Nifty trick."

Kyrie flipped, easily stealing Fen's position. A wicked-looking smile stretched Kyrie's lips. "I've got more where that came from."

Fen's groan was out of his control. He had a feeling it was about to be a long night. His suspicion was confirmed when the lube ended up used on his asshole.

"Well, this is a position I have nae been in, in a verra long time."

Kyrie didn't stop toying with Fen's body while kissing Fen's stomach. "You like it, though. I see that in your mind."

Fen definitely couldn't deny it. He just hadn't been sure Kyrie would.

Kyrie froze. He met Fen's stare. "We have an eternity together. There's nothing I don't want to try with you."

Dirty images filled his head. Flash after flash had his cock leaking in desperation.

Kyrie didn't stop filling Fen's head with every naughty scene imaginable as he pushed his way inside.

Fen's body not only accepted him, but it also tried to greedily suck him deeper.

Kyrie gasped. His pleasure slammed into Fen's. Fen immediately came. So too did Kyrie.

Kyrie panted through the waves but kept thrusting—never taking mercy on Fen. Fen loved it.

"It's always best we get that first orgasm out of the way."

Kyrie burst into laughter. His eyes shone bright with mirth. Like that, Fen had never been more addicted to anything in his life than this flawless soulmate he had been handed. Fen didn't doubt they still had secrets and long stories ahead to work their way through, but he never wanted them to leave the bed again. Maybe they wouldn't.

Keep your eye out for the next Devilish, *Unmated.*

About the Author

CHARITY PARKERSON IS AN award-winning and multi-published author with several companies. Born with no filter from her brain to her mouth, she decided to take this odd quirk and insert it in her characters. One of her greatest loves is writing morally gray characters. You'll find them scattered throughout her hundreds of titles.

*Nine-time Readers' Favorite Award Winner

*2015 Passionate Plume Award Finalist

*2013 Reviewers' Choice Award Winner

*2012 ARRA Finalist for Favorite Paranormal Romance

*Five-time winner of The Mistress of the Darkpath

Connect with her online:

*Sign up for her newsletter: https://bit.ly/charityparkersonnewsletter

*Join her readers' group on Facebook: http://bit.ly/CharitysTribe

*Website: https://www.charityparkerson.com

*A list of her social media accounts and giveaways all in one place: http://hy.page/charityparkerson